**every
third
thought**

other titles by john barth

JOHN
BARTH

• • • • •

every
third
thought

a novel in five seasons

COUNTERPOINT

BERKELEY

Library of Congress Cataloging-in-Publication Data

Barth, John, 1930-
 Every third thought : a novel in five seasons / John Barth.
     p. cm.
  ISBN 978-1-58243-755-2
 1. College teachers--Maryland--Fiction. 2. Life change events--Fiction. 3. Life
cycle, Human--Fiction. 4. Coincidence--Fiction. 5. Visions--Fiction. 6. Eastern
Shore (Md. and Va.)--Fiction. 7. Psychological fiction. I. Title.
  PS3552.A75E94 2011
  813'.54--dc22

                                    2011012434

Paperback ISBN: 978-1-61902-012-2

Cover design by Faceout Studio
Interior design by www.meganjonesdesign.com

COUNTERPOINT
2560 Ninth Street, Suite 318
Berkeley, CA 94710

www.counterpointpress.com
Printed in the United States of America

for Shelly

contents

pre-amble:

CLEARING GEORGE I. NEWETT'S
NARRATIVE THROAT

"YOU DON'T KNOW about me," Samuel Clemens kicks off "Mark Twain's" *Adventures of Huckleberry Finn* by having Huck declare to the reader, "without you have read a book by the name of *The Adventures of Tom Sawyer*."

Likewise, Reader, you don't know about *me* "without you have read" a little short story series called *The Development*, having to do with life in the once-upon-a-time mid-to-upscale gated community of Heron Bay Estates, on Maryland's Eastern Shore, in the quarter-century between its construction in the 1980s and its near-total wipe-out in the late afternoon of October 29, 2006, by a fluke tornado in the otherwise all but storm-free hurricane season that ended with those devastating few minutes. The seventy-seventh anniversary, it happened to be, of the calamitous stock-market crash of 1929 that ushered in the Great Depression of the 1930s, and one more reason why a certain Has-Been (Yours Truly) came to be who he currently is.

In Huck's case, the chances were that the "You" he addressed in 1884 would at least have heard of, and quite likely even have read, his tale's popular forerunner of 1876. A century and a quarter later, the odds are that You knew a thing or two about Huck Finn even before first opening any of his author's books, so popular an American icon has that boy-on-a-raft deservedly become despite his narrative's rough initial critical reception and its author's neglecting to account for semiliterate Huck's ability to sustain a 250-page first-person spiel addressed to "You." No such luck in my case—let's not go into that—and so permit me to introduce myself. "G. I. Newett" here, Reader, his name in wincing quotes for reasons no doubt to be explained although perhaps already obvious: self-styled Old Fart Fictionist and, until his academic retirement some years ago, professor in nearby Stratford College's pretty-good/not-bad/quite-OK Department of Literature and Creative Writing. Wherein his indispensable wife and soul-mate—the pretty-good/not-bad/quite-OK poet-professor Amanda Todd—still does her teacherly thing between stanzas, so to speak, and spins out her poetry (sorry there, Mandy: *crafts her verses*) between class and academic committee meetings, just as her longer-winded mate, in semesters past, used to spin out his All But Futile Fictions while coaching StratColl apprentices in the clearing of their own literary throats.

Never heard of us? You're excused. Being me, more or less, I'm tempted to say, "Gee, I knew it," but the puny pun would be lost (good riddance), in the unlikely event of its translation. As will another to follow, central to the tale that "G.I.N." aims to tell if he ever gets its shit together and his own.

Which, begging Your leave, he and "I" shall now re-attempt, if and while and as best we can:

More or Less Fresh Start

What most bothers Yours Truly—George Irving Newett, with whom Reader is unlikely to be acquainted from having perused his scant and minimally published scribblings—is not so much the psychophysiological fallout from his Accidental Head-Bang in the late afternoon of September 22, 2007, although it could certainly turn out to be more than trifling. For if "Pride goeth before a fall," what cometh after? Hairline skull-fracture at one's former hairline? Intracranial pressure from subdural hematoma, leading to chronic headache and even (as shall be seen, or at least imagined) hallucinations? Loss of one's already ever more fallible memory along with one's already age-impaired hearing, eyesight, libido, and general life-zest? We'll cross those bridges when and if G. comes to them, if he hasn't already without our realizing or remembering his having done so. Meanwhile, what we-all most fret at (Mandy too, fellow teacher and wordsmith that she is) is the ham-handed *symbolism* of his/my falling, perhaps in more senses than one, on *the*

first day of fall—which moreover happened that year to co-
incide with Yom Kippur, the Judaic Day of Atonement! As if
Adam and Eve's fateful fall from grace had occurred on the
autumnal equinox, and they'd lost their fig leaves just when
the trees of Eden were about to shed theirs! G.I.N. would never
have let one of his wannabe story-makers get away with such
clunky symbolic coincidence back when he was coaching the
Stratford workshoppers with one hand, teaching World Lit 101
with the other, and vainly hunt-and-pecking his own fictive fol-
lies with some presumable third—"vainly" meaning to quite
limited avail, successwise, inasmuch as years of polite editorial
rejection had early shorn him of authorial vanity.

Did Eden, come to think of it, even *have* seasons before
that "fall in which we sinned all"? Wasn't the Expulsion from
the Garden an expulsion out of timeless, seasonless Paradise
into time, self-consciousness, mortality, and the rest? What's
more, that primordial couple's "fall" occurred in the springtime
of their lives, so to speak, and *began* both their sexual history
and human history in general. . . . So hey, the Author of Genesis
could maybe use a bit of symbol-adjustment, too: like Yours
Truly, perhaps a better hand at coaching others to clean up
their acts than at cleaning up His own?

In any case (as if all the foregoing weren't heavy-handed
enough), get a load of this: Just as the tornadoing of our Heron
Bay Estates community fell on the seventy-seventh anniversary
of the Crash of '29, so G.I.N.'s 2007 bean-banging fall day/
Yom Kippur fall happened to fall on the faller's seventy-seventh

birthday! Nor are we done yet (Muse forgive the shameless Author of us all!): It was on the first anniversary of that first-mentioned mini-apocalypse—the *yortzeit*, as it were, of Heron Bay Estates, a bit more than a month after his birthday trip-and-tumble—that George Irving Newett, just beginning to imagine that he might after all escape any further fallout from that fall beyond a small scar in mid-forehead like a Hindu caste-mark, experienced the first of what has turned out to be (thus far, at least, as afore-feared) five serial, seasonal, vertiginous, and extended . . . *visions*.

Yup: one dream/doze/vision/trance/transport/whatever per subsequent North Temperate Zone season through calendar 2008, we're embarrassed to report, more or less coincident, after that initial five-week-late one, with each season's inauguration-day, and each having to do with some pivotal event in the corresponding "season" of the visioner's life. Nor is even *that* the end of our Clunky Coincidences. . . .

Aiyiyi! If we were making this story up, even G. I. Newett would pack it in and hit DELETE. But facts are facts, as best we can reconstruct and report them—including hallucinated-or-whatever "facts"—and so here we by-George go, with apologies to Aristotle, for example, whose *Poetics* famously recommend to us storytellers the Plausible-Even-If-Perhaps-Strictly-Impossible over the Possible-But-Bloody-Unlikely, if push comes to shove in that department. Apologies too to South Temperate Zoners, whose seasons fall in different quarters of the calendar from ours, with correspondingly opposite connotations to

"April," "September," and the like; ditto Tropics-dwellers, all
but seasonless except for Wet and Dry. . . .

I give up.

But not undiscourageable G.I.N., who, instead of DELETE,
here clicks once again the signature key to every self-disrespect-
ing O.F.F.'s career and to the lives of us still-traumatized Heron
Bay Estates tornado-survivors:

RESTART.

first fall

L AST FALL—I.E., AUTUMN 2007, or more exactly the run-
up to that September equinox—it being about to be G.
I. Newett's afore-specified birthday, he long since out to pas-
ture from Academia and his wife enjoying a last well-earned
sabbatical leave before her own retirement, the couple treated
themselves to their first-ever cruise-ship cruise: eight days on
the Baltic and North Seas (Stockholm/Copenhagen/Dover, with
intermediate stops and shore excursions) followed by a week
ashore in England and culminating, on G.'s birthday, in our
first-ever visit to William Shakespeare's birthplace in Stratford-
upon-Avon. Motives obvious, over and above much-needed respite from the reassembly of our storm-smashed lives: couple of
long-time English profs, both of whom routinely included bits
of the Bard in their undergrad lit-survey courses (George mainly
the plays, Amanda the sonnets, neither of us with scholarly authority, but both with the appreciative awe of fellow language-
fiddlers). Add to that the Stratford/Avon connection: Our joint

employer, as you may have heard, is a thriving two-century-old
liberal arts college in the even older colonial-era customs port of
the same name in Avon County, on Maryland's Eastern Shore
of Chesapeake Bay, where the towns and counties have English
names (Salisbury, Cambridge, Oxford, Stratford, Chestertown,
Dorchester, Talbot, Cecil, Avon, Kent) and the numerous tidal
waterways are still called by names predating the Brits' arrival:
Chesapeake, Nanticoke, Choptank, Sassafras, and Stratford's
own winding Matahannock. What's more, while neither G.
Newett nor A. Todd attended StratColl as students, the writer
of these lines was born and raised in Stratford town—more pre-
cisely, in the crab-and-oyster district of Bridgetown, a rough-
and-ready working watermen's ward divided from Stratford
proper by narrow, wharf-lined Avon Creek. Which waterway
ebbs and flows into the Matahannock River, which does likewise into Chesapeake Bay and thence <> Atlantic Ocean, <>
Bristol Channel, <> lower Severn River (*Britain's* Severn, not
Maryland's over by Annapolis), into which flows one-way >
the non-tidal upper Severn, its upstream reaches fed in turn >
by the River Avon. Which is to say (so Mandy informed me on
location) "River River," *Avon* being the Celtic word for same.
Although none to our knowledge has ever done so, one could
imaginably *sail* Stratford-to-Stratford, setting out from one of
the wharves near "our" Stratford's old Custom House (or from
late lamented Heron Bay Estates' once-upon-a-time Marina
Club), working downriver and down-Bay, hanging a left at
Cape Charles into the North Atlantic, crossing it northeastward

to the U.K., and forging thence upstream to where the original Avon flows through its original "Strait Ford" (i.e., narrow crossing), the eponymous town on its northwest bank. Across from which, by George, and connected thereto by a modest bridge, is the original Bridgetown!

Who knew?

Not us Newett/Todds; nor did we make that happy discovery by doing a Captain John Smith in reverse and sailing from Chesapeake to Channel, New World to Old. Instead, we drove Mandy's high-mileage, pesto-green Honda Civic through intermittent late-summer-afternoon showers from "our" Stratford (i.e., from the rented riverside condo in which we'd been making shift since Heron Bay Estates' doomsday) up I-95 past Wilmington to Philadelphia Airport's long-term parking lot and shuttled therefrom with our baggage to the terminal. Cashed one traveler's check into Euros, tsked at the once-almighty dollar's declining value, and boarded a Scandinavian Airlines A300 Airbus for the overnight economy-class flight to Sweden. A quite decent complimentary in-flight dinner, to our pleasant surprise, with champagne available at $5 U.S. per split, served at 10,000 meters (so the cockpit announcement informed us) above the already dark ocean. We treated ourselves to a brace of splits, toasted our survival, our much-blessed union, and our well-earned (and by Mandy well-planned) vacation; then sipped, nibbled, read, held hands, and dozed through the long, cramped flight, wishing we could someday fly first class, but impressed by how relatively more comfortable and better served we were than on the several long-haul U.S. airlines we'd used for earlier trips abroad, earned with frequent-flier miles from our credit card accounts. *Adíos*, American Century; *hasta la vista*, USA! Safely landed after a *very* early breakfast for our maiden visit to Scandinavia, we reclaimed our luggage, cleared customs, and were duly met by a cheery/brisk cruise-line rep holding up two signs, one reading NEWETT/TODD and the other HADLEY (a large Pennsylvania couple also booked for the voyage). Were by him Volvo-vanned through a sunny-mild Swedish morning to the cruise-ship docks, the jet-lagging four of us admiring en route the handsome busy city: so many bicyclists pedaling to work in their office clothes, a thing rarely seen back home, and everything so *clean*!

Hefty, red-faced Tom Hadley, his accent more deep-Southern than Pennsylvanian, supposed to our driver, "Reckon y'all don't have the *mi*-nor'ty problems we Amurkans have."

"Or else you keep your panhandlers and drug dealers out of sight," his wife teased. "Wish *we* could!"

"Or just maybe," my Mandy suggested to the backs of their heads from our rearmost seat before our smiling driver could reply, "a more equitable economy, a better health-care system, and more enlightened drug laws do the trick."

Without bothering to turn around, "Yeah, right," Hadley growled: "Plus taxes through the kazoo." We Todd/Newetts exchanged knee-nudges; I contented myself with opining that the correct idiom was *out* the kazoo, not *through* it, that term being a slang euphemism for the you-know-what.

Whereof, we agreed later, these particular fellow "Amurkan" tourists were prime specimens. But our professionally courteous driver-escort merely winked into the rearview mirror and declared in flawless English, "We Swedish have slang terms, too—and here we are, ladies and gentlemen! Enjoy our city and your cruise!" For we had indeed turned out of charming, canal-veined Stockholm proper into its port area and specifically its busy cruise-ship docks, where half a dozen sleek, enormous vessels were tied up. By local time it was still only mid-morning; inasmuch as our ship's embarkation was scheduled for seven that evening, and boarding not permitted before two in the afternoon, we tipped our driver, checked our bags as instructed at the loading area for delivery to our stateroom, and set out map in hand to explore on foot, per Mandy's pre-planned plan, the nearby canal-side streets, shops, houses, and sidewalk cafés, pausing at one of those last for lunch and hoping we'd be able to stay clear of the Hadleys aboardship in the days ahead.

Because while we had enjoyed a bit of small-boat day-sailing in decades past and were no strangers to foreign and domestic travel, *cruise-ship* cruising—as may have been mentioned?—was not something to which we had thitherto been inclined, and that not simply because of the expense. A Volkswagen camper, backpacks, and Frommer's *Europe on $5 a Day* had been our style back in the late 1960s (our early-professorial twenties and thirties); rental cars and modest hotels thereafter, through our less cash-strapped forties and fifties and on into our sixties. We were small-time academics, not CEOs! In the long summer vacation-time, when not wrestling with our separate muses we liked poking about the cities, towns, and countrysides of our nation and others on our own, not in guided tour-groups; enjoyed getting lost, asking directions, coping with languages and local customs as best we could, following our guidebooks' tips for lodgings and eateries within our budget. As a rule we preferred a country's streets and plazas, parks and coast-roads to its museums and castles, and when touring the latter, inclined to do so at our own pace, not in a docent-guided tour group. And we had little taste for "nightlife" beyond an after-dinner stroll, if we still had legs enough at day's end, before turning in. What use had the Newett/Todds for what we imagined to be the confines and enforced sociability of a cruise ship crowded with hundreds of fellow tourists? A cramped lower-deck "stateroom," pre-set dinner hours and seating, bridge tournaments and on-deck shuffleboard, nightly stage productions, and the constant tipping of room-stewards and other functionaries—not our style.

Until accumulating years began to make the prospect of on-our-own touring ever less appealing, to G.I.N. at least— been there, done that—and the accumulating resources of our modest lifestyle (two incomes, no dependents, adequate pension and medical benefits from our professorships at the College, plus a not-insignificant legacy from Amanda's parents, who'd had more savvy than George's in the estate-planning way) led Mandy to check out alternatives for her upcoming academic leave. After a bit of asking around among friends and colleagues and a *lot* of Internet chat-room research, "PrimeTime Cruise

Lines *Seven Seas*," she announced in September of '06, over wine and hors d'oeuvres on the screened porch of our second-floor Blue Crab Bight "coach home" in dear old Heron Bay Estates: "Stockholm to Dover this time next year, with stopovers in Gdańsk, Copenhagen, Amsterdam, and Bruges. Eight days aboard ship with no constant packing and unpacking, no scrabbling around for hotels and restaurants! King-bed stateroom with balcony! Three onboard dining rooms to choose from, with no pre-set dinnertimes! Eat by ourselves or with others as we wish—and no tipping! Then from Dover we take a bus or train to Canterbury, London, and Stratford–upon-Avon and say hello to Chaucer and Master Will—unless we feel like renting a Morris Minor, driving on the left, passing on the right, and shifting gears left-handed: your call. And after Stratford we fly home from Heathrow. Whatcha think?"

"Well, now," her bowled-over husband responded when he could: "As the Bard himself might put it, *Wowee,* and thankee thankee thankee! Maybe on location we can even nail down the difference between Stratford-*upon*-Avon and Stratford-*on*-Avon!"

Itself worth the cost of the expedition, smiling Amanda agreed, but then confessed as we clinked congratulatory wine-glasses, "Already did that, actually, on the Web: *On* is the district in Warwickshire—pronounced *Worricksher*?—and *Upon* is the town itself. Okay?"

"Okay! Did Professor Newett mention that he remains the humble and devoted servant of Professor Todd?"

"One suspects he did—and what she requests of said vassal just now is his meticulous review of all the shore-excursion and other cruise-crap stuff that she'll be dumping shortly on his desk." Another wineglass clink. "Happy seventy-sixth, *Giorgio mio!*"

For it was indeed in the near neighborhood of that anniversary, if not necessarily on its very date, that she announced this ambitious project, on which she had been laboring quietly, Amanda-style, for weeks. It would be, as she'd warned, more expensive by far than any previous junket of ours: The cost of its trip-cancelation insurance alone would almost have covered one of our early campground-and-youth-hostel expeditions to Iberia or the Canadian Rockies. But what the hell, we were Tenured or Emeritus Old Farts these days, with who could say how few healthy life-semesters remaining and no offspring to be benefacted. And as he expected, G.'s follow-up review of A.'s extensive research quite supported her enthusiasm for the plan, especially its Stratford-to-Stratford aspect. From StratColl's "Shakespeare House" (whereof more presently) to the Bard's actual once-upon-a-time domicile (ditto): Anchors aweigh! PrimeTime Cruise Lines being a justifiably much-in-demand operation, we locked in our reservations with a whopping year-in-advance down payment.

Whereupon the goddamn gods, as if to demonstrate yet again that their heavy-handedness knows no limit, exchanged winks at Mandy's "*Giorgio mio*" and saw to it just a few weeks later that the seventh named tropical storm of that year's season—yup, *Giorgio*—would spin up from the Caribbean and shift from tropical storm to hurricane strength and back as he passed under Puerto Rico, whacked hapless Haiti, crossed Cuba and the Florida Straits, and moved close offshore up the southeastern USA to his next landfall at Carolina's Outer Banks, thence into the mouth of Chesapeake Bay and usward up the Delmarva Peninsula. Where to our premature vast relief he showed every sign of fizzling into mere more-or-less-severe thunderstorms and much-needed rain, the way most of G. I. Newett's O.F. Fictions fizzle in the second or third trimester of their gestation. Except that (and how G. wishes *he* could pull off some narratively equivalent surprise, for a change) one of those t-storms, as if to give the finger to us Vastly Relieved Heron Bay Weather Watchers, farted out *en passant* the afore-noted short-lived but violent F3 tornado that miraculously killed only a couple of our number but quite destroyed the exurban gated community of Heron Bay Estates, including the over-and-under coach homes of its—of *our*—Blue Crab Bight subdivision.

Our library! Our home-office files and work in "progress," such as it was! Not to mention furniture and clothing, photo albums, and other irreplaceable souvenirs of our decades to-gether, no more than half of it salvageable (unlike many other buildings in the development, our particular duplex was left standing, but its windows, doors, and half the roof were gone with the wind). Ourselves physically unharmed, we happening to be on campus at the time—Mandy in her office in StratColl's Shakespeare House, the modest frame-bungalow headquarters of the Creative Writing Program, and Yrs Truly looking up something-or-other in the college library-stacks when shit hit fan—but our so-agreeable routine life *kaput.*

Not the cheeriest kickoff to one's seventy-seventh year and the half-time of one's partner's sixty-fifth. Through the remainder of that academic semester and into the next (from ingrained habit, we Todd/Newetts think of a year as divided primarily into fall semester, spring semester, and summer break, and only secondarily—or for particular literary purposes—into seasons), as with our fellow Heron Bay refugees we salvaged what we could of our belongings, scrabbled and scrambled to set up housekeeping in new quarters (less of a crisis, though still a major headache, for the more affluent with already-established second homes elsewhere, but a particular problem for us middle-income single-homers, "exurban" to a small college town in a semi-rural county with limited available housing), we more than once considered scrapping our proposed and already down-paymented Stratford-to-Stratford adventure. How afford such an extravagance now with so many unanticipated expenses straining our budget? And what was that costly trip insurance for, after all, if not to cover our butts in unexpected setbacks like this? Wardrobes to be replenished, salvaged possessions to be put in storage until we found new permanent lodgings, insurance adjusters to be negotiated with—and for Mandy, classes to be taught as well, lectures prepared, and papers graded! Not to mention bye-byes to our separate, not-all-that-busy muses. Anchors *away* (until some next life, maybe). . . .

But rather to our own surprise, after lucking out of our post-Giorgio motel-squatting into a well-furnished riverfront condo in Stratford (leased from a history-department retiree who'd recently moved with his wife to Florida and might even agree to sell if they decided to remain there) and making shift in office-space at the college—Mandy in her official departmental quarters, G.I.N. at the desk of an ex-colleague on leave—while setting up our new home work-spaces and negotiating a reasonably reasonable insurance payout on our total-loss Blue Crab Bightery, by mid-spring we found ourselves managing not badly, all things considered. Well enough, anyhow, to begin looking forward again to that upcoming September PrimeTime Cruise Lines fling as a welcome, well-earned reward for so much cataclysm-coping. After which—who knew?—we might even get back to doing some Creative Writing ourselves instead of merely supervising its apprentice creation by others. Anchors aweigh? Especially since, as Mandy discovered and reported, trip cancellation because of financial setback resulting from natural disaster was not covered by our travel policy?

Anchors aweigh, and off we by-George went, as afore-reported, by car and plane from tidewater Delmarva to Sweden's handsome capital; strolled same with pleasure until embarkation time, admiring its quaint old Gamla stan byways while giving the figurative finger to its Swedish Academy for never having awarded their Nobel Prize in Literature to such now-late worthies as Vladimir Nabokov, Jorge Luis Borges, and Italo Calvino—each of whom would have done at least as much honor to the prize as it to them—while often bestowing it instead upon writers whom even we lit-lovers may scarcely have heard of, and many of whom, to put it mildly, must lose a *lot* in translation; then boarded that sleek palazzo of a cruise ship and were escorted to our stateroom, duly impressed en route by the elegant atriums, wide staircases, glass-enclosed elevators, and endless amenities, including a bouquet of fresh flowers and an ice-bucket of champagne awaiting with our already-delivered luggage. We unpacked, agreeing that our quarters were every bit as commodious and well-appointed as advertised, and then convened with fellow passengers in the main ballroom for a welcome-aboard orientation/reception (more champagne and hors d'oeuvres) followed by lifeboat-drill and, if not the literal weighing of the vessel's anchors, the casting off of its mighty dock lines, the revving up of its sun-dry side-thrusters (no tugboats necessary these days, we were told, in most instances), and the *Seven Seas'* departure from Stockholm's harbor into the Baltic.

The history-drenched Baltic, new to us Newett/Todds, who though no strangers to the Mediterranean, Aegean, Adriatic, Tyrrhenian, and other European seas and/or seacoasts, had never till now ventured upon this one, a favorite for summer-time cruisers. Their typical itinerary, Mandy had explained back home long since, would be from Stockholm to Estonian Tallinn, thence up the Gulf of Finland for an extended stop-over in St. Petersburg, then back to Helsinki and other ports, sailing mainly by night and shore-excursioning by day (a welcome respite for cabin stewards and suchlike shipboard service personnel) until the voyage's end in Copenhagen. But pleased as we'd have been to tour the canals and onion-domes of Dostoevsky's *Crime and Punishment*, she had elected instead to fetch us from Stockholm straight down to Polish Gdańsk (with an interim stopover at the charming medieval island-port of Visby), thence west to Copenhagen, Amsterdam, and on to Shakespeare Land.

And that's enough traveloguing: Suffice it to say that thanks to Mandy's homework and judicious planning we quickly shed our reverse-snob cruise-ship prejudice and quite enjoyed both vessel and voyage. Disembarked at Dover's famed white cliffs, vowing to Do This Again Sometime down our road—maybe on the same just-right-for-us ship (neither overwhelmingly large, like some of the super-behemoths one saw in harbor, nor small enough to enforce intimacy with the likes of those Hadleys), maybe from Dover down the coasts of France and Portugal and on around Iberia to Nice or Monte Carlo, once the pair of us were pensioners? Were met dockside by driver prearranged by M. and by him fetched through rolling, sheep-flocked Kentish countryside to Canterbury, which Chaucer's tale-telling pilgrims never quite reach in his uncompleted *Tales*, but we T/Ns duly did. Regained our shore-legs among the half-timbered houses and the great old cathedral, paying our respects to Geoffrey C. both as poet and as talester: no Failed Old Fart he, despite his failing to fetch his fictive folk to their destination! Then bypassed London, whereto we'd be returning anyhow for the flight home, and contrived somehow by bus, train, and taxicab (ask Mandy) to haul our tandem tushies and assorted luggage up to Warwickshire's Stratford-on-Avon and Stratford-upon-same, which is where this long-stalled story (finally!) starts. . . .

On a certain mild but drizzly, quite English-feeling late September Saturday morn—first day of fall and seventy-seventh anniversary, as has been noted, of George Irving Newett's expulsion from maternal womb in Bridgetown, MD USA—he and his soul-mate wake in their somewhat cramped but cozy bed-and-breakfast in Stratford-upon's Bridgetown, make happy birthday love in its (too small for us Amurkans) double bed, "break fast" with good Brit tea and scones, and, thus properly B&B'd, set out under borrowed umbrellas across the B'town-to-Stratford bridge into "Upon," as we'd come to call it. Being us, we decline the "Shakespearience" guided tour of the Bard's birthplace, later residence, and final resting place in Holy Trinity Church, preferring to touch those bases at our own unsupervised clip. We happen to be, both of us, *literal* touchers of stuff that we venerate: not paintings, of course, but items unlikely to be damaged (in our opinion, if not that of museum-guards and tour-guides) by the odd respectful body-contact. In Spain, for instance, touring the Cervantes residence-museum in Alcalá de Henares some decades past, G.I.N. had presumed actually to sit at what was advertised to be the master's desk, his butt in the very chair that Don Miguel was said to have honored with his while penning *Don Quixote*, and had felt as moved thereby as a True Believer might feel at touching the bronze robe-hem of a patron saint's statue. Likewise Amanda, back there in Canterbury, had caressed the granite walls of the cathedral right through a beautiful Evensong recital, paying homage not to Gee-dash-Dee but to the splendid architecture, music, and other art inspired by His various religions—along with Crusades, Inquisitions, Jihads, and the like. To the objection that even such respectful, reverential touching does damage over time, we reply with what we once overheard a fellow tourist remark at the sight of a famous old crucifix's marble Jesus-toes worn down by the kisses of the faithful: "If lips can do that to stone, think what stone must do to lips!"

An example of which, changes changed, will now befall (perpend that verb) the writer of these lines. Down Stratford's handsome Henley Street we make our way, the small rain dampening everything but our spirits, to the large half-timbered house where on or about 23 April 1564 (St. *George*'s Day, by G.!, though the exact date is uncertain) the Master drew first breath—Mandy per usual missing nothing en route, and her mate per usual busy with the tour-guide reading and travelogue note-taking that in Her opinion distract him from seeing much of what we're there to see, but in His preserve a range of details for our future reference, from the number of our favorite room in Canterbury Lodge to those musical numbers so beautifully rendered by organ and choir at that aforementioned Evensong. And it comes to pass that with his attention thus divided—one eye as it were on the guidebook page describing the house immediately before them, the other on the object of that description, and his depth perception thereby at least metaphorically impaired—G. I. Newett misjudges the building's unusually high stone entrance-step, missteps up thereonto, loses his balance, overcorrects, stumbles and slips or stumbles back and down, and then falls forward, map and guide- and logbook flying as he tries in vain to catch himself, and bangs his forehead squarely on that step-edge, incidentally scraping left palm and right elbow, and bending but not breaking his rimless eyeglass-bridge.

Exclamations of alarm from wife, from entryway ticket-taker, and from tourists of sundry nationalities before and behind the faller! Who picks himself up, saying, "It's okay; I'm okay," while checking with Mandy to see whether in fact he is. Together they discover not only those incidental damages but—of more concern and potential consequence—that his step-banged brow is now bleeding profusely down under his bent eyeglass-frame and over his nostrils to his lips and chin (like many another oldster, G.I.N. takes a blood-thinning daily aspirin along with his vitamin/mineral supplements as a deterrent to clots and strokes, and therefore bleeds more freely from scrapes and cuts than one would otherwise). "I'm *okay*," he tries again to reassure her, hoping and more or less believing that he is, on (recovered) balance, or anyhow will be once the forehead-gash, stanched for the nonce with a wad of pocket Kleenex, is properly cleaned and bandaged.

Nothing more than a basic first-aid kit available on the premises, its much-concerned docent informs us, but there's "a proper chemist just a few squares off." His assistant fetches the kit, which we make use of in the visitors' WC while he goes back to ticket-taking and she to tour-guiding. The bleeding retarded but not altogether checked by a couple of gauze pads, and the gash itself not really sterilized, we decide to postpone for a bit our planned salute to Will's nativity on George's natal day and detour instead to that pharmacy, whose obliging on-duty "chemist" not only sells us a supply of appropriate-sized bandages, but at no charge inspects the wound, cleans it with antiseptic swabs before re-bandaging it himself, and declares that in his judgment it requires no sutures, but offers to direct us to the nearest National Health Service facility if we want it checked out by a regular physician.

"We really ought to do that," opines Mandy, and George sort of agrees, but really *really* doesn't want to: The thing's not hurting much now; the bleeding seems to be under control; his slightly bent eyeglass-frames prove readily re-bendable almost to their former alignment. Later that day, at their B&B or wherever, we'll re-clean and re-re-bandage; meanwhile, he'd much rather get on with what we've come so far to see and do. Back to Henley Street and environs, okay?

"What do *you* think?" she asks the so-obliging pharmacist. He cocks head, shrugs, winks, and allows that's about what *he'd* do in our shoes, though his missus mightn't. He warns, however, that serious head-bangs can sometimes have delayed consequences—intracranial hemorrhaging and the like?—and so at any sign of dizziness, headache, whatever, I should get myself promptly to a clinic.

Agreed. And more or less worrisome as is that possibility, we manage after all a most pleasant birthplace/birthday tour, returning to mid-Henley Street's landmark Jester statue (starting place for most walking tours of the town) and thence to the Birthplace, taking care this time at that high entrance-step. Greeted familiarly by the ticket-chap, who compliments G.'s considerably tidier though already somewhat bloodstained brow-pad, we mount the also-steep staircase to the building's first floor and tread the very floorboards once toddled by the baby Bard, then move out and on to Bridge, High, and Chapel Streets, the eight-century-old Old Town, Shakespeare's grave, and the lovely Avon river- and canal-side walks, pausing here and there to change the bandage, eat lunch, take a piss, or merely be moved by such proximity to the man Mandy calls "King of the Queen's English" and by the haunts of his erratic domestic life: married at age eighteen to twenty-six-year-old Anne Hathaway (already three months pregnant), upon whom he fathers two more children and *from* whom he then flees to make his career in London, but *to* whom he more or less returns in his prosperous early retirement and famously bequeaths his "second best bed" upon dying on his fifty-second birthday.

Which this present 'umble servant of said sweet language managed *not* to do on his after-all-well-spent seventy-seventh. Leg-weary but much satisfied with our salvaged day, at its afternoon's end we return to our modest lodging not far from the bridge to Bridgetown (a very different-looking venue from G.I.N.'s birthplace of the same name in Maryland's merely 300-year-old Stratford—but then, it too has much changed over the decades since this scribbler drew first breath: from a rough-and-ready watermen's village squeezed between the riverside crab-picking and oyster-shucking establishments and Stratford's segregated Negro ward, to a still downscale but gradually integrating sub-community showing such signs of gentrification as a yachting marina, a passable seafood restaurant, and a row of new waterfront condominiums where the old commercial packing-houses used to be). Once again we clean, disinfect, and bandage the still raw and bruised but no longer bleeding brow, then change into warmer wear and stroll to a previously-checked-out nearby pub to raise mugs of good brown ale over shepherd's pie and suchlike Brit vittles.

"Happy happy happy happy happy," bids Poet/Professor Amanda Todd, and as if suddenly inspired by that pentametric salute, goes on to rhyme: "*Were your wife a bard Bardworthy instead of crappy, / She'd sing our lucky love from bed to verse, / And make from her sow's-ear talent some silk purse.* Amen—so to squeak?"

"Hear hear!" applauds her grateful O.F.F. "And had your mate been the yarn-spinner you deserve, right-thinking readers would be dissing Stockholm for not giving *him* their effing prize. But his *real* complaint is that he has no reason to complain." Never mind fame and fortune, he goes on to explain to her, not for the first time: He only wishes he'd managed to perpetrate in her honor a gen-you-wine Capital-N Noteworthy Novel or two over the past half-century. "Your hubby's a fucking failure, luv. Cheers?"

Well, now, replied ever-loyal she: Come to that, at two years past the three-quarter-century mark he remained a still-*fucking* failure, anyhow, as his drying-up old rhymer of a mate could testify from that morning's pre-breakfast frolic. To us, then, damn it, and our good luck with each other if not with our muses or the high step up into Shakespeare's-'hood? And on with whatever's to be the next episode of our (still-) fucking story?

Aye aye, ma'am. And even as this account of that fateful fall day has shifted from present back to past narrative tenses, so now shall our quite successful September tour. Never mind its close in big busy history-drenched London and big *too*-busy Heathrow; the long flight back to our Bush/Cheney-afflicted U. S. of A.; the jet-lagged drag of clearing customs, claiming baggage and long-parked car; the bleary-eyed two-hour drive from Philly to that Stratford-Come-Lately on the Matahannock, changing G.I.N.'s brow-bandage only twice a "day" now insofar as we could reckon days. We made it, just as we'd made it through the latter half-and-then-some of the Terrible Twentieth Century into the quite possibly Terminal Twenty-First: no kids or grandkids, unlike Will and Anne (although we sometimes *pretend* to have them: more on that later, I'd guess); no recently-published prose or poetry, nor any of our prior pubs still in print—but thus far no cancers/strokes/ Alzheimer's/etc. either, nor (thus far) serious aftereffects of the fall. And decades of well-taught classes, well-critiqued student papers, well-colleagued colleagues, well-read books, and well-traveled trips to take satisfaction in. . . .

And overlong catalogues like the above to be done with already, for pity's sake! Back to our "pre-trip" routines (and bemused by the extra voltage on that adjective as we laid upon friends and colleagues our travelogue and its culmination in G.'s Henley Street trip-and-fall), we relished our new perspective on *our* Stratford, *our* Avon (County), *our* Bridgetown (whereof more to come, Muse willing-maybe-please?). Before each after-noon's errands, chores, desk-business, and recreation, we went as usual each weekday morning to our separate workrooms in hope of inspiration, and as usual . . .

Well: As usual, September sang its song and became October. In synchrony with Delmarva's agribusiness feed-corn harvest, the migratory geese returned in strung-out V's from Canada and honked along our Matahannock, bringing with them brisk cool-weather fronts to relieve Tidewaterland's drought-stressed but blessedly hurricane-free summer and re-mind local "snowbirds" that it was time for them to shift south to their winter HQ's in Florida. As StratColl's fall semester got under way, the fine maples, oaks, sweetgums, and sycamores on campus and along the town's streets showed first signs of au-tumn color. Ideal weather for end-of-season yard work (if one owned a yard) and the battening of hatches for cold weather to come; for the year's maybe-final bicycling, or canoeing and kayaking from the college's waterfront facility; for enjoying the long late light with sips and nibbles on porch, patio, or pool deck before November's chilly shift back to Standard Time, and for savoring one's own autumnality before winter comes. "Can't last, of course," one acknowledged over clinked wineglasses: neither good weather nor good health nor one's happy though less-than-ideally-productive life with mate nor for that matter the nation's already-overstrained economic prosperity and the planet's dwindling natural resources. The "American Century" was already behind us, followed by those quagmire wars in Iraq and Afghanistan, an alienated international community, a declining dollar and rising energy costs, Gilded Age excesses and inequities, climate change, economic recession— the list went on (and on and on, as G.I.N.-lists tend to do). *Meanwhile*, however?

Meanwhile, the news media busied themselves with the upcoming 2008 U.S. presidential election—the primary campaigning for which was gearing up already a full year in advance, both parties relieved that the Incumbent could not succeed himself for a third term in office—and the Newett/Todd muses sat on their Parnassian butts (the Newett one, anyhow: Mandy, more indifferent to Her output-rate than George to His and more shrug-shouldered about publication, prefers to keep her poetical musings pretty much to herself). In the weeks following our return from abroad, even as his very slight headachiness dissipated and his brow-wound healed to where no further bandaging was required, G. found himself preoccupied to the point of obsession with that fall/fall/Yom Kippur/birthday co- incidence and its Adamic echoes, of which he was inescapably reminded every time he looked in the mirror to shave, floss his teeth, or check his attire.

"I think the wench is trying to *tell* me something," he'd report at morning's end. "Like those mumbling monsters in the old Hollywood horror flicks."

"So stay tuned," recommended Mandy. "Me, I've got a class to teach, a batch of papers to grade, and a hung-up villanelle-in- the-works to straighten out in my spare time."

Been there, done that, changes changed: *Arrivederci*, love, and Muse be with you while Hubby turns with relief to such ac- complishable after-lunch tasks as vacuuming the floors, picking up as many of the items on our grocery list as he can with con- fidence as the house *sous chef*, and then re-meeting her at the campus tennis courts for an hour of mixed doubles (sweatsuited against a cool late-afternoon breeze off the river) with another pair of StratColl-connected Heron Bay Estates refugees. With whom, between sets, we'd shake our heads at the approaching first anniversary of our erstwhile community's destruction and compare notes on our intentions with respect to it. The younger, more vigorous Simpsons—Pete an associate dean at the col- lege, Debbie an associate librarian—whose home in H.B.E.'s detached-house Rockfish Reach neighborhood had been sorely damaged but not altogether wrecked by T. S. Giorgio's tor- nado, were already busily rebuilding an improved version of it and helping to plan a new, ecologically "green" Heron Bay Estates, but were concerned that the downturn in the nation's housing market and the upturn of its mortgage-foreclosure rate, while not yet damaging to them personally, might well put a freeze on the development's redevelopment.

Us?

Damned if we knew, we shrugged. Much as we had enjoyed our nearly two decades there, we doubted whether we had interest or energy enough this late in our day to rebuild on our own initiative. If some general contractor re-did our "old" Blue Crab Bight neighborhood (an unlikely prospect in the present slump), perhaps we'd re-buy there in what was becoming ever more a buyer's market. More likely we'd just sit tight in our rented condo; maybe buy *it* if its Floridian owners chose to unload at a duly modest figure.

"Unless our B.M. Move comes first," one of us would interject at this point: H.B.E. slang for its older residents' not-uncommon next-to-last relocation across the Matahannock to the same developer's Bayview Manor Continuing Care facility. After which, the grave. And *meanwhile*, as G. I. Newett believes he was saying?

Meanwhile, he'll forge in the smithy of his head-banged but not yet quite fossilized fancy one more effing O.F. Fiction, by George, this one having to do with, let's see . . . fall-falls? The autumnal equi-knocks of a tottering talester seasoned by life's seasons? By *his* life's seasons: its Spring, its Summer, its Fall, and fast-approaching Winter? . . .

Thus maundered he, while Amanda repaired her villanelle (so she would report somewhere later) and the couple's mortal days ticked by to 29 October 2007, the eve of the eve of All Hallows Eve. In Stratford and environs, a day not unlike those just before and after: nearly warm enough for shorts in the afternoon, then cool enough that evening to light the condo's gas fireplace while attending the usual cheerless news from Pakistan, Afghanistan, and Iraq despite the White House's rote reassurances that our recent troop "surge" was making progress. To our home and/or campus offices after breakfast; to our classes/chores/whatever after lunch. After dinner, an informal anniversary-memorial gathering of H.B.E. survivors organized by Dean Pete and Debbie Simpson in one of the college's function-rooms borrowable for town/gown occasions, whereat the disaster's only fatalities (a couple about our age, crushed in the rubble of their faux-Georgian house in Rockfish Reach) were duly saluted and other storm-trauma memories shared, along with decaf coffee and differing opinions regarding the development's future. And after *that*, back "home" to enjoy our pre-bed time in customary Todd/Newett fashion: an hour or so of separated reading (Mandy comfortably chaired in the condo's guest-bedroom-cum-improvised-home-office with a new biography of her beloved Emily Dickinson, G.I.N. couched before the afore-lit fireplace with some young upstart's deservedly acclaimed first novel), followed by a reunited, port-wine-nightcapped hour of video entertainment (in this instance, the DVD'd first half of one of Jane Austen's alliteratively titled, social-class-driven, handsomely filmed *chef d'oeuvres*: *Pride and Prejudice*, was it? *Sense and Sensibility*? Manors and Manners, anyhow), followed by a bedtime goodnight embrace and, for Yrs Truly, about two hours' sleep before the first of his thrice-a-night old-fart get-up-and-pees—followed finally by what this long fanfare has been snail's-pacing toward. Having made his way from night-lighted bathroom through darkened *boudoir* and climbed back into their bed's His side (on his mate's right, in our right-handed household, so that when the couple turn to each other his "good" arm is uppermost, free to caress . . .), he found himself suddenly overwhelmed by a strange, strong, out-of-nowhere *vertigo*, followed by

DREAM/VISION/TRANSPORT/WHATEVER #1

A sort of prolonged flash: no "action," but an extraordinarily alive 3-D not-quite-still shot, with all senses operating. Wintertime sunset over brown frozen marsh and gray expanse of open water, viewed from fixed position well above scraggy loblolly pines. No people in sight, but Viewer (stationary) feels . . . accompanied. *Also distinctly feels frigid air on face, and both sees and hears stereophonic strings of geese and ducks out over marsh—some below eye level. Overall sensation stirring, even mildly exciting in its vividness.*

End of "vision": G.I.N. waked or revived flat on back in dark bedroom beside slumbering spouse, head feeling a bit odd still, but rapidly normalizing. Wondered *What the fuck?*, shaken not by vision's unalarming content (generic tidewater scene, unusual only in its oddly elevated viewpoint), but by its startling clarity and full sensory accompaniment on the heels of that brief dizziness—a vertigo not felt in the "dream" itself and now all but cleared, so he guessed he wouldn't bother Mandy with it unless and until (Zeus forefend) something like it recurred. In which case, he promised himself, he would duly consult the Todd/Newett primary care physician. His Upon-Avon Shakespeare House fall was, after all, five symptom-free weeks behind him. . . .

No recurrences, thankee thankee thankee Z., at that night's second and third urinations, with normal sleep and normally half-coherent dream-fragments between; nor any the next day and night, nor the next and next. One gratefully presumed therefore that one was out of the woods, concussionwise if not musewise, and returned to one's futile workday-morning fiddling with that fall/fall/life-seasons stuff, accumulating page after page of notes on this and that aspect or possible significance, week after week while the world ground on and mortal time ticked by. Leaves fell, as did the U.S. housing market and the Dow-Jones Industrial Average. First frosts froze. Thanksgiving, first snow flurries, Pearl Harbor Day, and first light snow accumulations (short-lived) as autumn ran its run and the days shortened toward winter solstice.

Equinox. Solstice. Equinox. Solstice. "Bitch is *definitely* trying to tell me something," our man re-reported presently to his Mandy—with whom, of course, he had shared his peculiar,

all-but-actionless "vision" (minus its preliminary vertigo) in the
hope that her 20/20 poet's eye might see more in it than his pro-
saic and bifocaled ones had managed to. But all she could offer
was "Maybe if you invoked your personal Parnassian more politely?" So "Prithee, Ma'am?" he begged in effect through mid-
December, returning in daily vain to his brief written description (in italics, *supra*) of that all-but-actionless though curiously
happy-feeling winter marsh-scene.

And then one day, as we Once-Upon-a-Timers get around
to saying one way or another—Friday 12/21/07 it was, in fact:
just before the solstitial noon—as George Irving Newett entered
StratColl's own unassuming Shakespeare House* to meet his
Mrs. in her office and do lunch together in a nearby pizzeria,
the low step-up over a wooden doorsill from its screenless,

---

* Headquarters of the college's Creative Writing Program, as ought to have
been mentioned earlier but may or may not have been, at least in the present
narrative-in-utero. The modest frame bungalow just off campus with its offices, workshop/seminar rooms, and student lounge area was purchased some
decades ago with a generous endowment from a wealthy alumnus who in
his college years had aspired to playwriting, but who made his considerable
fortune as CEO of Tidewater Communities Inc., the developer of Heron Bay
Estates and other projects. The ever-increasing interest on that endowment
not only maintains our Shakespeare House, but also funds our program's little
literary periodical (*The Stratford Review*), pays for a series of visiting reader/
lecturers each semester, and notoriously subsidizes our annual student literary
award, the almost embarrassingly large Shakespeare Prize. For more on this
problematical plum (on whose judicial committee both of us Newett/Todds
often serve, doubtless earning us the same scornful finger at times that one saw
G.I.N. give the Nobel committee some pages back), Reader may either wait
for Narrator to amble back to that subject, as chances are he will, or check
out an item called "The Bard Award" in that story series mentioned in the
"preamble" to this ramble.

almost ramshackle front porch into what had originally been the bungalow's living room and was now an informal student lounge area reminded him (for the first time, oddly) of the high stone entrance step of that *other* Shakespeare House, where on a certain previous seasonal-division day . . .

And *that* reminded him—how hadn't it occurred to him long before?—of when/where/how, as a kid, he had first been made really aware of solstices, equinoxes, and the like. The sudden recollection literally dizzied him: less than the lead-in to that afore-italicized one, but enough so that—excusing himself to skinny male undergrad in black warm-up suit on much-worn sofa just inside lounge—he sat down beside him to steady himself before climbing the stairs to Mandy's second-floor office.

And noticed that although the kid was perusing *USA Today*, the magazine he'd picked up from the cushion beside him and plopped onto his lap to make room for the couch's new occupant was—Get *outta* here!—the Jehovah's Witness illustrated monthly *Watchtower*. And under it (now likewise lapped), the old Everyman edition of Shakespeare's comedies. . . .

"*¡Jesu effing Cristo!*" he'll groan to endlessly patient Mandy over Bozzelli's pepperoni/mushroom pizza after collecting himself and her for their lunch date. "I feel like I'm living in the kind of greenhorn novel that I might've perpetrated at that kid's age if I hadn't had my old buddy Ned Prosper to rein me in! Where are you when I need you, Nedward?"

"Have another slice before it gets cold," is his wife's advice, "and tell me all about it between mouthfuls."

As best he could, he did, and was so possessed by the recounting that—again at her suggestion, but he needed no prodding—instead of doing whatever he'd had in mind for that afternoon, he returned to the workroom in which he'd spent another all-but-eventless morning, refilled his ever-ready Montblanc Meisterstück with Parker Quink, and (*sans* vertigo this time) first-drafted the following.

SOLSTITIAL ILLUMINATION OF POST-EQUINOCTIAL VISION #1:

The Watchtower

21 December 1936, it will have been: the depths of the Great Depression, but a frosty-bright late afternoon in tidewater Maryland. Light snow cover as afore-envisioned, but no ice on the roads, and nearly no wind. On the prickly-plush rear seat of Mr. and Mrs. Prosper's big black LaSalle sedan with its handsome whitewall tires (including spares nestled into each front fender; no tire-chains needed today, but there's a set in the trunk, just in case), Narrator is comfortably ensconced between, on his right, first-grade classmate/buddy Ned Prosper, and on his left Ned's three-years-older sister Ruth. It's a birthday-party excursion, unlike anything Narrator's family could ever imaginably come up with: Ned having been born on the winter solstice of 1930, and Narrator on that year's autumnal equinox three months prior, the Prospers—newly moved to Bridgetown from across the creek in Stratford—have decided to celebrate the occasion by driving over to marshy South Neck, on the Chesapeake Bay side of Avon County, to climb the new fire-watchtower erected there by President Roosevelt's Civilian Conservation Corps (special permission from the local CCC having been secured by Mr. Prosper, a Democratic county commissioner as well as principal of Stratford Junior High School), and to watch the sunset of the year's shortest day from the windowed observation booth at the tower's top, saluting its descent below the western horizon with mugs of thermos-bottled hot chocolate and specially-baked birthday cookies. All hands are decked out in winter togs: galoshes, scarves, lined gloves, stocking caps, sweaters, and warmest jackets. Corduroy knickers and knee-socks for the boys; woolen leggings beneath the ladies' skirts. In the front passenger seat, trim Mrs. Prosper, an English teacher at the private Fenton School outside Stratford (which Ruthie will attend instead of the county's public schools when she reaches ninth grade—or "First Form," as it's called at Fenton), keeps up a merry banter with the youngsters, in which her husband also joins. Through the half-hour cross-county drive, brother and sister play Cow Poker by the complicated Prosper Family Rules, with centrally-seated Narrator as scorekeeper and Mom and Dad as referees: Not only are the pastured cattle on each player's side of the road counted and added to that player's score, with half their value to be subtracted from whoever's side the LaSalle happens to pass a gas station on, but double credit is given if the player correctly identifies the breed as Ayrshire, Guernsey, Holstein, or Don't Know (meaning that the Referees don't know either; if they do, one point per head instead of two), and there are

*further complications as well, all administered in high-spirited
mock solemnity. Winner to go first behind Dad Prosper in the
upcoming Great Watchtower Climb. . . .*

Even to a callow first-grader, the contrast with Narrator's own
family was stark. Fred Newett—sometime insurance salesman,
sometime car salesman (he'd arranged the Prospers' purchase
of that LaSalle), and sometime other things—was never an *un-
kind* father to his only child, just an impassive, distracted, and
not very interested one, no doubt in part because of the double
burden of the nation's economic and his wife's psychological
depression. Aside from whatever might have been Lorraine
Irving Newett's congenital disposition and any marital problems unrecognizable by a six-year-old, she had been much sad-
dened by the stillbirth of her and Fred's first child (a girl, two
years pre-George) and the late-term miscarriage of their third
(another girl, two years post-). While declaring herself quite satisfied with her son, she made no secret of her disappointment
at not having a daughter as well. "It would've been so *nice* [her
signature adjective] if you'd had a sister. Wouldn't that've been
nice?" Narrator supposed so; what did *he* know? The Prosper
siblings bickered and teased good-naturedly, and since the boys'
kindergarten friendship they more and more included Narrator
in their high-spirited taunts and tussles, which he quite enjoyed.
While he didn't really *mind* returning home to only-childhood
and his comparatively indifferent parenting—Dad buried in
his newspapers and desk-business after a long day's whatever,

Mom busy in kitchen or sewing-room or working crossword puzzles in her front-porch rocker and inevitably replying (as when Narrator later recounted to her this adventure-still-in-progress), "Now wasn't *that* nice!"—the contrast didn't escape him. Dave and Mary Prosper were forever attending or hosting dinners, club and church and school events, outings with their friends and their children's friends; the Newetts, while cordial to their Bridgetown neighbors, had almost no social life.

"Here's how we're doing it, mates," Dad Prosper instructs them when all hands pile out of the LaSalle at the fenced-in base of the steel-truss watchtower, at least a hundred feet tall, surrounded by pines and underbrush on a dirt-and-oystershell road halfway down South Neck: "How many of us are there in this birthday climbing-party, Nedward?"

Pretending to count carefully, "One, two, three, four, five!" the birthday-boy replies; then teases, "Unless Gee doesn't count?" His nickname for Narrator. "Or I count twice?"

Nay to both propositions, the parents agree, clever Ruthie adding however that if both of those silly propositions were true, the answer would still be five.

"Attagirl!" applauds Mom, while Narrator is still sorting out the arithmetical logic. And, "Look carefully now, Georgie-boy: How many pairs of platforms must we daring climbers climb before we reach that tower's top? Count every second platform."

"One, two, three, four, five, six, seven, eight, nine, ten . . . five pairs?"

"Quite a coincidence, hey? And at each of those second platforms, we climbers are to pause and gather 'round. Am I right?"

"What for?" wonders Ned. The rest of us grin knowingly and say nothing.

"And the order of the ascending climbers shall be: First,"— Mr. P. indicating himself—"the heaviest member of the troupe, to make sure the CCC's construction job is sound. Second, the winner of our hard-fought Cow Poker match, its contestants neck and neck until that Texaco station in Rock Harbor cost the birthday-boy half his herd."

"Booo!" jeers the loser, while his sister triumphantly curtsies.

"Behind and below her, our Guest of Honor . . . " Ned's turn to bow. "Followed by . . . our Honored Guest." I.e., Theirs Truly, honored indeed to be included in that happy clan, though unable to articulate his gratitude. "And tailed closely in turn by the organizer-in-chief of this valiant adventure, whom we here applaud."

We duly do, while pretty Ma Prosper mock-curtsies like her daughter and warns us not to count on her to catch us if we tumble, she being an acrophobe who'll be clinging to the stair-railings for dear life.

"Acrophobe?" Narrator wonders aloud.

"Look it up, Dummy," suggests Ruth.

"But while you're looking it up," Ned adds, "Don't look down."

All hands laugh, Narrator included, who doesn't yet un-
derstand the joke but recognizes that there is one, and does
understand his friend's whispered follow-up advice: "Look up
Ruthie's dress instead!"

"Naughty naughty!" his sister scolds, who's anyhow wear-
ing those cold-weather leggings. Her dad having opened the pad-
lock with borrowed key, through the gate and up the first steep
flights of metal stairs we go in designated order, gloved hands
gripping the stair rails, four-fifths of us rehearsing silently, as we
climb, our respective parts in the little five-step ceremony that
Ned's parents have devised without his knowing it. At the first
"second platform," Mrs. Prosper calls out, "Landing Number
One!" Then she gathers us together, holds up one forefinger,
points the other at her wondering son, and declares in a loud
singsong: "When he was one year old, he was wetting the bed!"

"Was not!" Ned protests, but "Were so," his sister smugly
affirms.

"Onward and upward, and enough of that," directs Dad.
Pausing us next at "Landing Number Two!" (i.e. platform four)
he picks up his wife's singsong: "When you were two years old,
you were walking, Ned!"

"And talking a blue streak," adds Mom.

"And messing with my stuff already," adds Sis.

"I think I'm catching on," the birthday boy groans. "Let's
get this over with."

But "Not so fast, young man," his mother says, and in-
structs us all to appreciate the changing perspective on our

surroundings from the successive platforms. "Like the way we get a better view of things as we grow up," she explains: "ourselves included." To which her husband adds, "It's what's called an incremental perspective, okay? Try that one on your teachers sometime."

And indeed, by the next even-numbered platform—where Ruthie, in her turn, announces, "Landing Number Three!" and then recites to her brother, "When you were three years old, I was six already, so nyah!"—the assembled are approaching treetop height, and Narrator is wondering already whether on Maryland's table-flat Eastern Shore and in low-rise Stratford/ Bridgetown, where few if any buildings are more than four stories high, he has ever been farther off the ground than he'll be at . . .

"Landing Number Four!" he calls out when they've climbed there, per their secretly pre-rehearsed program; then adds, in rhyme with the verse before, "When we were four years old. I didn't know you yet, Neddy."

"Boo-hoo," the Guest of Honor sarcastically responds, whereat Narrator musses his buddy's cap, and Mr. Prosper instructs us to notice the muskrat houses out in yonder marsh and to appreciate that if the CCC and the Park Service hadn't recently declared this whole area a National Wildlife Refuge, its valuable wood- and wetlands would be being deforested, drained, and turned into farmland like so much of the rest of our peninsula, without regard to the environmental consequences.

"The what?" Ned wants to know, and his parents explain.

"But when you were *five* years old," Mrs. Prosper recites at "Landing Number Five!"—*the last platform before the tower-top observation booth*—"you two were kindergarten friends. . . . "

"And now you're *six* years old!" *we choristers then proclaim in unison, one of us at each platform-corner and the eye-rolling birthday boy at its center.* "And here's how your birthday poem ends:

> *Happy birthday to you,*
> *Happy solstice day too!*
> *May you prosper, Neddy Prosper,*
> *When the winter is through!"*

"Wow," allows he, quite obviously wowed as his family hugs him while Narrator looks enviously on. Then "Better get ourselves aloft now," Mr. P. advises, "if we want to see what we've hauled all this way to see. Same climbing-order, please, and do be careful"—the final, shorter ascent being no angled stairway, but a vertical metal ladder leading to a narrow walkway around the booth. His sister thus positioned directly above his head as we climb, Ned calls out "We see Christmas!" even though, for the aforementioned winter-wardrobe reasons, we don't. Nor had Narrator ever, except for a few fleeting instances on playground swings and seesaws, seen up a girl's skirt to her thus-designated underpants, not to mention—what Pal Ned claimed his sister had displayed to him more than once, and what in

*the season to come, up in the Prosper family attic, she'll offer
for Narrator's Let's-Play-Doctor examination—the bare-naked
Mystery itself.*

"*Boys . . .* " *tut-tuts Mrs. P.*

"*Will be boys,*" *her husband supposes, standing by at the
ladder-top to hand each of us safely up onto the walkway.
"Looks like we're just in time and might even luck out with the
clouds. Remember not to look directly at the sun till it's almost
all the way down, okay?*"

*Had Narrator ever even seen a proper sunset before?
Certainly not such a view of one, from such a viewpoint. The
great Chesapeake itself—"Largest estuarine system on the
planet," Mrs. Prosper informs us, having first defined* estuarine *"for any who mightn't know"—is visible to westward beyond the snow-patched marsh-grass and loblolly pines; a few
last workboats are motoring in toward Rock Harbor, and
Maryland's western shore—which Narrator had seldom set
foot on, but the Prospers often ferried over to, to Annapolis,
Washington, and Baltimore—can be made out on the far horizon. Toward it the great orange sun has already descended to an
altitude of no more than one Solar Diameter (term supplied by
Ned, who some minutes later will officially announce, "Lower
limb touching!" and bump his left leg against Narrator's right).*

*Despite Dad Prosper's warning, what youngster could not
steal furtive glances aplenty as the grand disk first touches the
hazed horizon and then steadily sinks behind and below it, its
movement perceptible for the first time in Narrator's life? "And*

remember," Mrs. P. reminds all hands, "it's not the Sun that's moving, but us: the Earth spinning on its axis from west to east." A literally dizzying idea, at that height and in those circumstances: Narrator grips the platform-rail to steady himself as, with parental permission once the sun is two-thirds set, they attend its final disappearance, hoping to see the legendary green flash reputed to occur under just the right atmospheric conditions at sunset's last moment, but which none present has ever witnessed.

"I think I saw it!" ventures Ned.

"Did not," declares his sister.

"Maybe on Birthday Seven?" either Mom or Dad offers, and the other says, "Time for us to go down now, while there's still light to see by. Hasta mañana, O sole mio, and pardon my French." And on the merry ride back to Bridgetown, amid the back-seat/front-seat banter and more talk of solstices and equinoxes, "Just remember what the Good Book tells us," Mr. Prosper mock-solemnly bids all hands: "To every thing there is a season."

"Ecclesiastes Three," footnotes his wife, who teaches kids' Sunday School at Bridgetown Methodist-Protestant Southern.

winter

2

ND THERE ENDED "Gee's" *Solstitial Illumination of Post-Equinoctial Vision #1*, as he seems to have dubbed his first-drafting thereof. No green flash at *its* close, either—when with gratified relief he transferred it from loose-leaf binder to desktop computer, editing as he typed—but an afterglow of further associated memories, not all of them warm. Such a contrast between his old pal Ned's family life and his own! ("Now wasn't that *nice*," Mom Newett granted, scarcely looking up from her dinner plate of Smithfield ham, steamed kale, and mashed potatoes while he recounted his adventure; and Dad once again disdained such "three-initial make-works" as CCC and WPA: "We Piss Anywhere," he would sniff at the sight of road- and bridge-builders standing about.) That last line of Ned's birthday song, *When the winter is through*, reminded G. now not only of the heavy literal winters of his childhood—snow forts and snowmen and snowball fights under the leafless maples of Bridge Street; the creeks and rivers frozen hard

john barth

enough for ice-skating, and even the Bay itself ice-locked at times from shore to shore, as almost never happens nowadays; coal bins and coal furnaces in those years before most folks switched to oil or gas; even free-standing wood- and coal-stoves in the houses still without central heating—but also of the long economic winter of the Great Depression, more burdensome to *his* parents, he came to understand, than to Ned and Ruth's, who were on the state payroll. As Fred Newett more than once dryly observed, "Schoolteachers mightn't get paid *much*, but at least they get paid *regular*."

"And that means something," G.'s mother would agree, characteristically not troubling to explain to her son just what, in fact, it meant: the security of knowing that however much the family might have to scrimp and save while FDR's New Deal gradually improved the nation's general welfare, at least they wouldn't likely be standing in breadlines or squatting in "Hoovervilles" like so many of their less fortunate countrymen.

"Et cetera," G. concluded now to *his* wife, who supposed she was lucky to have been born twelve years after her spouse— just in time for World War Two?

"Another grim season," her husband granted, although he could still hear his father declaring (probably over Chesapeake crabcakes, coleslaw, and iced tea, another favorite Newett family menu) that it sure put the country's economy back on its feet, their domestic one included, despite wartime short-ages and rationing: his insurance business up; people eager to buy new cars—or better used ones, as war production raised

48

farm and factory incomes but curtailed production of non-essential goods.

"*Seasons*," Mandy echoed. We happened likewise to be enjoying crabcakes, made however with blue-crab meat imported from who knew where, the local crabbing season having ended in the fall; and instead of iced tea we sipped jug Chablis and mineral water. "You seem to be hooked on that particular motif lately."

Netted by, he guessed he'd say, rather than *hooked on*, the accompanying victuals being crustaceans rather than fish. But, "I reckon I am: hooked in spades, to mix another metaphor." Because the more he mused it—which is what he mainly did with his mornings through that January and February and into March, while Senator John McCain won the Republican presidential primaries, and Senators Hillary Clinton and Barack Obama battled each other for the Democratic nomination, and things dragged bloodily on in Iraq and Afghanistan, and the stock market went down and up and down, but the price of food and fuel went up up up—the more it appeared to him that those ascending levels of the South Neck fire-watchtower, with their "incremental perspective" of the surrounding scene, could be said to correspond not only to the successive years of his and Ned Prosper's then-so-young lives, but also to the successive stages, or extended "seasons," of Narrator's much longer Story Thus Far. The first of which ("Platform Number One!") might be thought of as the Depression-era "Winter" of their Bridgetown childhood. Ages zero through thirteen, say: birth to adolescence. Or better, kindergarten through "junior high," as middle school was called back then: the period of "Gee" Newett's developing buddyhood with (the late) "Nedward" Prosper, whose never-published (because never finished) *magnum opus* this "seasons" thing ought properly to have been and might somehow yet manage to become, if Ned's old and still aging pal can bring it off.

The late . . . We'll get to that.

"So you're hooked. Netted. Hung up. Whatever," said Poet/Professor/Helpmeet Amanda Todd. "So haul in your catch, even if it's yourself. As your friend's parents said back in 1936 and Pete Seeger sang in the 1950s, *To everything there is a season*, right? Me, I've got Shakespeare's sonnets to teach tomorrow morning and their author to learn from tonight, so if it's okay by you we'll do the dishes now and I'll join you later."

We did that, as is our custom: cleaned up together what we'd together prepared and enjoyed, then withdrew to separate rooms, not this time for our usual postprandial hour or so of undistracted leisure reading, but Wife instead to work in Her makeshift home-office workspace, and Hubby—most unusual for him at this hour—to do likewise in His: to make a few reminder-notes, at least, of some further Kids-in-Bridgetown recollections triggered by his "vision" of that long-ago fire-tower climb. E.g.:

—*Their high-spirited street and sidewalk games*: "Gee," "Nedward," Ruthie, and a couple of Ruth's girl friends, maybe. *Hopscotch*, played with oyster shells tossed onto the chalked diagram. *Jump rope*: the girls only, as he recollects, but he and Ned sometimes spun the longer rope for them, duly calling "I see Christmas!" if occasion warranted. *Kick the Can*: rules forgotten, but not the satisfaction of being first to reach the empty quart-sized food tin standing inverted in mid-Water Street (the low-traffic side road on which both families lived, just off busier Bridge Street) and send it clanking down the macadam, sometimes under a parked car. Backyard *Hide-and-Seek*—or Hide and *Go* Seek, as they customarily called it, perhaps preferring the rhythm of that extra syllable; or Hide and *No* Seek, as they'd call it when whoever was "It" decided as a prank to go sit on the front-porch steps and wait with amusement for the hiders to realize that they weren't being sought—with one of the neighborhood's great maples (all now dead and gone, like the original residents of its two-storey clapboard houses) designated as Home.

—*Fishing* (apropos of his and Mandy's recent talk of his "being hooked" and "hauling in the catch") in Avon Creek with Ned and Dad Prosper, off the concrete seawall at the foot of the Bridgetown-to-Stratford drawbridge, a few blocks from their houses. No rods and reels for the youngsters, but long bamboo poles rigged by Mr. P. with hooks, lines, bobbers, and sinkers, and baited with bits of peeler-crab meant to snag, with luck, perch and "hardheads" barely large enough to be Keepers, but sometimes eels (a slimy nuisance to untangle and unhook) or inedible, bait-wasting toadfish, which one simply whacked to death on the seawall-top and tossed back. Although the Keepers generally yielded no more than a few forkfuls each,

Mrs. Prosper and even Ma Newett, when not in one of her
down spells, would obligingly scale, clean, pan-fry, and serve
them up for dinner, typically with cornbread, mashed potatoes,
lima beans, and her highest compliment: "Right nice."

—*Summertime swimming*, not in narrow and work-
boat-busy Avon Creek, but in the wider, relatively cleaner
Matahannock River, off a stretch of public sand-mud-and-
marshgrass "beach" above the point where creek joins river, just
downstream from the larger bridge connecting Stratford proper
to the neighboring county. More bathing and aquatic horseplay
than actual swimming, supervised in their early grade-school
years by Mrs. Prosper or a mother of one of Ruthie's friends,
later by Ruth herself, more or less, in her Big Sister capacity,
and on the boys' own from about age ten, by when the neighborhood deemed its kids capable of trekking unsupervised to
and from the rivershore as they did to Bridgetown Elementary,
and disporting themselves harmlessly through a sultry tidewater
afternoon. *No diving from the bridge*: a posted prohibition routinely ignored by the older boys. *Don't swim out farther than
you can swim back*: a rather self-enforcing rule; and *Stay out
of the main channel*: a more negotiable one, since work- and
pleasure-boat traffic was lighter on that upstream stretch of river
than on Avon Creek and the lower Matahannock, with its numerous other creeks, boatyards, and crab-and-oyster-processing
establishments. For these particular pre-teens, however, crawl-
stroking out to the river's channel would have bent, and perhaps
even broken, the preceding rule. *Watch out for skates and sea*

nettles: the former (a.k.a. sting rays) fortunately not numerous, and generally avoidable if one remembered to shuffle one's feet when walking on the firm mud/sand bottom (all but invisible in more than knee-deep water), but most unpleasant to be "stung" by—as witness Captain John Smith's near-fatal encounter with one off consequently-named Sting Ray Point on the lower Chesapeake during his first exploration of the Bay in 1608. The latter the less formidable though distinctly unpleasant medusa jellyfish *Chrysaora quinquecirrha*, so abundant in dry summers especially (when the brackish water becomes saltier) as to be all but unavoidable except by staying ashore.

Which, when the nettles were plentiful, the girls inclined to do, especially as they approached adolescence: a cooling dip now and then in the shallows just offshore, where they could more likely avoid being stung; then back to the more-or-less-sandy "beach" to play in its "sand" (not to be compared to the fine Atlantic beaches several hours distant, which the Prospers visited maybe twice per summer with "Gee" sometimes in tow), or merely stretch out on a towel like the older girls, gossip, leaf through magazines, and acquire a tan (more often a red, since only those older girls sometimes applied sun lotions, and SPF numbers weren't invented yet). Fair-skinned boys simply blistered, peeled, and got the bill some decades later in the form of actinic keratoses, basal-cell epitheliomas, sometimes even dangerous melanomas. Kids from Stratford/Bridgetown's Negro ward were luckier, Mrs. Prosper once observed, with respect to sunburn if little else. But one didn't know any of them personally;

they had their own small schoolhouse on the far side of town, and their own swimming-place somewhere down near the mouth of Avon Creek. To Ned and Gee and the other boys, the nettles were normally no more than a minor nuisance: In the water as much as the girls were out of it, the fellows romped and splashed one another, played Tag and Submarine, dived off the concrete bridge-piers and, as they got older, illicitly off the bridge itself— even *swam* a bit in the course of their horseplay, instructed by one another or the occasional parent. Their inevitable, more or less severe jellyfish stings (picric acid burns, actually, Mr. Prosper explained) they accepted like the skinned knees and scraped elbows from other sorts of play, and treated with various folk remedies: rubbing the inflammation with sand, which hurt so much worse that ceasing to do it helped a lot; pissing on it, if the girls weren't around and if the stream—preferably one's own rather than one's buddy's—could be aimed on target. To add one's uric acid to the medusa's picric, they would understand later, might be rationalized as fighting fire with fire; in any case, the fire always won. And now that we have their little weenies out . . .

—*Playing a different sort of "I See Christmas"* with Sister Ruth, not at the rivershore but up in the Prospers' attic at 213 Water Street, across and two down from the Newetts' 210. "Here we go," Narrator already imagines his mate sighing, to whom this tidbit will not be news: "*You show me yours, I'll show you mine*, et cet. What else isn't new? And who cares?" She and Sammy, she'll remind him [her two-year-older brother, killed in a Vietnamese helicopter crash back in the high 1960s] played Doctor a few times before they sprouted pubic hair, but does she write poems about it?

Why not, love? A Petrarchan sonnet, say, its Octave describing in memorable tropes the bold lad's "Jimmy" (or whatever you-all called it; that's what Gee's mom called *his* timid tool, when she needed to name it) and the sort-of-scared but not-uninterested lass's "Susie" (ditto, changes changed, and those blue-crab nicknames stuck); its Sestet the delicate—one hopes it was delicate!—hands-on inspection of each's by the other? In the case in hand, so to speak, all quite innocent, actually, as one hopes it was with the young Todd sibs: first the three D's (a Dare, a Display, a bit of Demonstration), then the four or five T's (Touch, Tweak, Titillating Tickle or Two). No harm done, and a thing or two learned, by Gee anyhow, up in that wintry attic among rolled-up summer rugs and stacked cartons in some appropriately literal Christmas season, 1939 or thereabouts: he and Neddy in maybe fourth grade, Ruthie in seventh, the three of them parentally dispatched to find a certain box of colored light-strings with which the Prospers (unlike the Newetts) traditionally decorated their screened front porch and entrance doorway. "Long as I can remember," saucy Ruth surprised them by announcing, "you guys've been saying *I see Christmas*, right? Well, take a good look, and then it's *my* turn." To the boys' considerable dismay then, she yanked down and stepped out of her step-ins (robin's-egg blue, as Narrator recalls, though he may be supplying their color from other, later initiatory experiences), hiked up her skirt, and thrust virtually into their faces the first female pudendum ever seen by George Irving Newett, almost though not quite too embarrassed to look. But "Look!" the bold girl demanded, and look they did: not merely at its ever-so-interesting frontal aspect (which didn't after all seem *totally* unfamiliar; Gee guessed he'd maybe seen photographs of nude female statues, but he didn't recall their having had that fascinating little crease up the middle), but at the between-and-under part as well, which she insisted they squat down and inspect close up—no poking, though, or she'd kill them both! They duly did, Gee at her orders not only *looking* at the curious pink puckers between her thighs, but (she gripping his wrist to guide and if necessary restrain him) lightly Touching, Tweaking, and Tickling them, as her brother was not allowed to do.

"Okay, now tit for tat: Let's see what *you*'ve got to offer." Her own undies snugly back in place, she knelt before them on the dusty boards, hands on her hips, and became the Inspector instead of the Inspected. The boys, having more than once ministered to their sea-nettle stings as aforenoted and enjoyed backyard pissing contests when no one was about, were not unfamiliar with the sight of each other's male equipment. To display it under present circumstances was a quite different matter, but they gamely did: unbuttoned the flies of their corduroy knickers and (avoiding each other's eye, but not a glance at each other's business) fished out their limp, pink-and-cream-colored little—

"*Penises*," Ruth Ellen Prosper declared, looking from one to the other with an expression of mild disgust. "*Pricks. Dicks. Cocks.* Now skin 'em back."

Do *what*? Ned Prosper evidently understood what his sister meant, and boldly obliged. Can it have been that George Newett at age nine remained unaware of the operation (never mind the names) of foreskin, prepuce, glans penis? Unlikely; but on a similarly wintry day nearly seven decades later, what he remembers is his having been too mortified to do more than stand there, pinching his penis between right-hand thumb and forefinger practically in Ruthie's face and wiping his suddenly sniffly nose with his left (on which—distinctly!—he caught the scent of *her* private parts from when their roles had been reversed) until, "If you're so set on seeing it," Brother challenged Sister, "peel him back yourself." Which to G. I. Newett's fascinated appall she daintily did: exposed for her close-up scrutiny what a dozen years later the then college-age pals, laughing and shaking their heads at the recollection over mugs of frat-house beer, would call "Rudolph the Red-Nosed Reindeer"* and then dismissing it with a finger-flick and a brisk, "Okay, you pass."

"Do I have to come up there and find that Christmas stuff myself?" Mr. Prosper inquired up the stairwell.

---

* Narrator's Google-search of whom informs him, among its two-million-plus entries, that the character of R the R-N R was invented by George May in 1939 as a marketing gimmick for Montgomery Ward Inc. and later turned into the song made popular by Gene Autry's recording in 1949, by when the Newett/Prosper boys will have begun their undergraduate years at Tidewater State University and Stratford College, respectively—Gee still floundering to find a major, Ned already on the verge of resolving to write the Great American Novel—and Ruth Prosper Garrett (a failing octogenarian widow now, Narrator understands, in the care of her daughter and son-in-law somewhere Out West) a newlywed Goucher College graduate whose "Susie" it was never his privilege to re-view.

"No need, Dad. We've got our hands on it right now."

So where am I? Ah, yes: at G.I.N.'s worktable all these winters later, making note of at least three more items from this early season of his and (the late!) Ned Prosper's story, out of the many prompted by that recent solstice-vision:

For starters, their early discovery of *books* as a source of extracurricular and sometimes even curricular pleasure. Those "Big Little Books," e.g.: hardcovers the size of half a brick, text on their left-hand 3" × 4" pages, black-and-white illustrations on their right, retailing the adventures of Dick Tracy, Tailspin Tommy, Tom Mix, Terry and the Pirates. Also a larger, radically abridged and expurgated edition of *The Arabian Nights*, handsomely illustrated by Maxfield Parrish. Plus innumerable comic books, more pictures than text, whose literally colorful depictions of Superman, Batman, and the rest drove Big Little Books off the market. And, as the pair graduated cross-creek from Bridgetown Elementary to Stratford Junior High and at Ned's parents' urging frequented the Avon County Public Library, the shelves of Edgar Rice Burroughs's *Tarzan* and Victor Appleton's *Tom Swift* novels. Stories, stories, stories! Much as they enjoyed watching Saturday-afternoon double features at Stratford's Globe Theater and listening to radio serials like *The Shadow* ("Who knows what evil lurks in the hearts of men? *The Shadow knows* . . . "), in those pre-television, pre-video-game days it was stories "told" in printed words that most appealed to them— the silent, privileged transaction between Author and individual

Reader (the boys regularly swapped books, but never read aloud to each other). Good old print: a shared early addiction that by their college years would become—unreservedly for Ned, half-hopefully for his sidekick—a calling, a true *vocation*. . . .

Second, Ned's habit already by sixth grade of proposing something—an illicit dive off the Matahannock Bridge, maybe— then saying, unless Gee said it first, "On *second* thought, we'll be in hot water if Ruthie squeals on us," and deciding finally, "On *third* thought, that damn water's too cold today: Let's go splash Ruthie and her friends instead." Or, on a wartime waste-paper-collection drive with fellow members of Bridgetown Boy Scout Troop #158, "Let's see what old man Thorpe [a local news dealer] has for us in this pile of stuff," and upon discovering therein a discarded trove of coverless *Spicy Detective* pulp magazines illustrated with line drawings of naked women in erotic peril, "On *second* thought, let's cop a couple of these for later," and having done so, "On *third* thought, to hell with the war effort: Let's go work on our Jack-Off merit badges." Whereupon, as the Nazis overran Europe, shipped its Jews off to extermination camps, invaded the Soviet Union, and poised to invade Great Britain, and as Imperial Japan, having surprise-attacked Pearl Harbor, extended its military dominion in the Pacific, Ned Prosper and George Newett practiced masturbation in the afore-described attic of 213 Water Street, the empty former woodshed of 210, and other secluded venues. It was his friend's "third thoughts," G.I.N. noticed early, that the pair most often acted upon.

And finally (regarding things Third and Last), Retired O.F.F.-Prof Newett is reminded of his Prosper-pal's predilection, even back then, for remarking Last Things, a habit that by his undergraduate years would become a virtual obsession:

"Last time you're gonna see *me* in these stupid corduroy knickers and kneesocks! *Long pants* from now on, or bare-assed!"

"Last ride on our dumb old junior bikes: Race you to the bridge, Gee!"

"Last day of Miz Brinsley's fifth grade. Boo-hoo! Whoopee!"

"Last week of vacation; better make the most of it!"

"Last year of President Roosevelt's second term!"

"Last day of the 1930s!"

"Last birthday before we're teenagers. Let's do Stupid Kid Stuff!"

"Better get some sledding done while we can: Last day of winter coming soon!"

Indeed. And almost seventy years later, as Senators Hillary Clinton of New York and Barack Obama of Illinois campaigned exhaustingly against each other to be either the first female or the first African-American presidential nominee, the winter of C.E. 2007/08 ran its unhurried, inexorable course, and at least two dwellers on Planet Earth began to wonder, vis-à-vis G. I. Newett's narrative-*in-utero*, "Just what the fuck *is* this, pray tell?"

Thus asked one of them, Poet/Professor A. Todd, of the other, her palms-up husband, who, as he not infrequently did, had requested that his mate please take a look at the paper-clipped pages that she now tossed back into his lap. Responded he, "That's what I hoped you'd help *me* figure out."

"Well, for starters, is it meant to be a novel or a memoir or what? How much of this silly stuff really happened?"

"Don't ask me; I just work here." Shrug. "Shit happens. And now I remember that I forgot to include a certain memorable First among all those Lasts." Namely, that it was on the afore-noted Last Day of fifth grade in Bridgetown Elementary that Yours Fictively George Irving Newett made his literary debut, in the form of a naughty poem about their stern, fat, and busty teacher. Scribbled in #2 Dixon Ticonderoga pencil on a torn-out sheet of blue-ruled composition-book paper as Miss Brinsley, standing before a large wall map, held forth on global time-differentials and the inversion of seasons between Northern and Southern Hemispheres, and meant to be passed surreptitiously over to Ned P. but noticed and pounced upon by its eagle-eyed subject before its recipient could finish reading it, Gee's *aabb* quatrain was spun off from an anonymous one considered funny by male Bridgetown fifth- and sixth-graders when shared orally at recess-time. The original:

> *Old Henry went to the burlesque show.*
> *He sat right down on the very front row.*
> *And when the girls began to dance,*
> *POP! went the buttons on Henry's pants.*

In Gee's longhand version:

Miss Brinsley sneaked into the burlesque show.
She sat way back on the very last row,
And when the boys began to cheer,
POP! went the snaps on her brassiere.

"Let me get this straight," now said Amanda Todd. "You're telling me that as late as 1941, at least a few fifth-grade boys in Bridgetown, Maryland, imagined that female sexual arousal involved mammary engorgement?"

"Some of us must've. What did we know?" What Narrator knew, and now reported, was that the formidable Miss Brinsley had been unamused. Crumpling the poem-script without expression and tossing it into her desk-side wastebasket (from which its author would manage later to retrieve it, he being assigned blackboard-erasure and trashcan-emptying as supplementary penance at that school-day's close), she had sternly summoned him to the front of the classroom, pronounced him guilty of indecency and illicit note-passing, ordered him to bend forward over the desk, and directed the poem's interrupted first reader to come forward and administer five hard whacks to the poet's posterior with a large wooden paddle kept prominently on display in a front corner of the classroom to discourage misbehavior. Why five? Opinions differed in subsequent playground discussion of the incident, some maintaining that it was one whack for each grade, others that it was one for each line of the already much-repeated quatrain plus one for good measure, and others yet that it was one for each snap-hook on Miss Brinsley's bra (more than the usual number, Ruth Prosper would inform us from her more knowledgeable perspective on such esoterica—but then, think of the size of Miz B.'s . . . *boobs*!). Author's punishment having been smartly delivered by Reader, at Subject's order the tables were then turned and three whacks laid by Scurrilous Sender upon Ready Recipient's backside, Miss Brinsley explaining to both and to the class that accessories to any misdeed, while perhaps less guilty than its perpetrators, must bear their share of responsibility.

In a put-on Eastern Shore drawl, "Sounds to me," Mandy allowed, "like yer ole Miz B. there was right smart of a teacher."

That she was, if a less than lovable one: She even explained to us the difference between Accessories Before and After the Fact. And we knew our Tropics of Cancer and Capricorn long before we discovered Henry Miller's naughty novels in college days.

"Which however I believe were first being published in France at just about the time you tell of. And what did Future Fictionists Prosper and Newett take away from this experience, other than sore *derrières*?"

Didn't hurt all that much, actually, in the physical way, and more of a scalding embarrassment to G. I. Newett, who knew he'd be in deep shit at home when word reached his parents, than to Ned P., whose folks, being educators themselves, were as a rule more understanding in the Classroom Mischief department. To all hands' surprise, however, there were no further unpleasant consequences. For whatever reasons, Miss Brinsley chose not to report the incident to either set of parents. Nor did Ned's sister "tell on them" when she quickly got chapter and verse, so to speak, through an extracurricular grapevine that extended from Bridgetown Elementary up through Stratford Junior High, where she was in eighth grade. She merely shook her head in disgust, promised much worse retribution than a mere handful of hiney-whacks to anyone who dared write such shit about *her*, and made the gossiped bra-hook-number correction mentioned above.

"You should know," one of us teased her—Gee, G. suspects, inasmuch as Ned was already remarking that a *handful* of whacks was exactly the right number: yet another possible explanation of the five-count.

"Don't think I'm going to show *you*," came back pert Ruthie, whose budding breasts, as far as Gee could judge, were not yet cupped: "Those peep-show days are in the attic for keeps."

"On *second* thought," Ned suggested on the school playground shortly after, where he and Gee and an approximate handful of their dodge-ball-playing classmates were yet again invoking what they'd come to call "the B.B.B. poem" (Brinsley/Burlesque/Brassiere), "shouldn't it go '*But* when the boys began to cheer' instead of '*And* when the boys' et cetera?" Not only because *but* adds yet another *b* to the line and the poem, he went on to explain, but because *but* ("Three more *B*'s, guys, get it?") better suits the sense of the situation: She "sneaks into" the burlesque show; she sits "way back in the very last row," not to be noticed—*but* the popping of her bra-snaps blows her cover.

"Not his exact words, of course," G. said now: "He and I are only eleven years old here, and people didn't 'blow their cover' back in 1941, and who remembers anyhow? What I *do* remember is that 'and/but' business, and agreeing that he was Right On (as we didn't say yet back then) about both the sense of the line and the alliteration—although of course we didn't know *that* term yet."

"In short," offered Ever-Helpful Spouse, "Fledgling Author and Fledgling Critic sprout their first feathers. I wish *I'd* had fifth-grade pals like you guys."

"Fledgling O.F.F. and about-to-fledge Capital-A Author," in her husband's opinion, "who alas had his wings clipped early. I wish *I'd* been your fifth-grade pal."

"Likewise. But when you were in fifth grade I was just getting conceived, and didn't know from bra hooks yet. I think I'm supposed to ask now: If that was your late buddy's Second Thought about your maiden literary effort (which I gather soon became your-and-his collaboration), what was his Third?"

Thanks for asking. If nipped-in-the-bud-novelist Ned Prosper were alive today to hear about George Newett's recent post-equinoctial vision and subsequent solstitial illumination, one can imagine his proposing on Third Thought that whatever else G.'s well-deserved fifth-grade paddle-whacks might be said to signify, they echoed also the five platform-stops of our birthday fire-tower climb back in first-grade days, of which the fifth and last before the tower-top had been declared to mark the inauguration of their friendship. "What he said at the time, however—unless I'm just dreaming all this?—was something like 'On *third* thought, Gee, that's the last time I'm getting paddled for being the damned Reader. From now on, whether I get whacked or whoopeed, I want it to be for my *own* scribbles, not somebody else's.' End of quote, paraphrase, misrecollection, whatever."

"And none too soon, in your helpmeet's helpful opinion. But if you're really doing this whatever-it-is, you might as well mention that that particular Third Thought of his was the first we've heard so far that's also one of those Last Things that you say he liked to make note of, if that happens to be the case. Excuse all those *that*s."

"May your grateful husband kiss your hand?"

"Whatever anatomical item he pleases. And before she *washes* her hands of this dubious enterprise, pray tell your ever-less-patient Reader what further relevance, if any, this extended naughty-poem recollection has to anything?"

Relevance? Ah yes, *that*. Well: Eight or nine years later, when Ned Prosper is a flourishing undergrad here at StratColl, and G. I. Newett is hanging on by his fingernails over at Tidewater State, and both are pretty much persuaded that their Capital-C Calling is the writing of Capital-L Literary fiction, Ned will enjoy maintaining that future lit-historians will trace the pair's epoch-making careers back to that initially humiliating but eventually inspiring day in Miss Brinsley's fifth grade, which introduced them to both the pains and the pleasures of literary creation. In his retrospective opinion, it will have been the B.B.B.-poem's subsequent notoriety, as it passed from furtively scrawled note into jointly revised and raucously repeated Playground Oral Tradition, that really fired both boys' passion not only for reading (especially *novels*: no longer Tom Swift and *Tarzan of the Apes* after elementary school, but Zane Grey's *Riders of the Purple Sage*, Jack London's *White Fang*, even Dumas *père*'s *The Three Musketeers* and *The Count of Monte Cristo*), but for *writing* made-up stuff: in Stratford Junior High, a satirical mock-Nazi underground "newspaper" called *Der Berlin Times* with crude cartoons of Hitler & Co., its handwritten single-sheet copies circulated among their classmates; in Avon County High, a pseudonymous gossip-and-humor column in the school's biweekly *AvCoHi Eagle* called "The Osprey," bylined *PN* (for Prosper/Newett, their joint "PN-name") and motto'd, "The *Eagle* soars; the *Osprey* pounces."

But that's another story: the blooming springtime of their teens and twenties and the American Century's '40s and '50s, following these Winter's-end first stirrings of their nascent sap, so to speak.

"Another *nom de plume* for the pair of you, maybe: *Nascent Saps?*"

Touché. And in the Here and Now, as the vernal equinox of 2008 approaches, Fidel Castro and Vladimir Putin at least nominally transfer authority over their respective domains to each's hand-picked successor; Hillary Clinton and Barack Obama still go at it in the early Democratic presidential primaries; the dollar slides; crude oil tops $100 a barrel; the Iraq war, then in its fifth year, costs the U.S. some $21 billion per month; the Taliban regains strength in our stalemated Pakistan/Afghanistan misadventure; severe late-winter storms strike California and the midwestern and northeastern states (but spare our mid-Atlantic Tidewaterland); and in early March a woman in Kansas is discovered not only to have been living secluded in her bathroom for two years, but to have remained seated so long on her toilet that the skin of her butt has grown literally attached to the seat, which must be removed before her discoverer/rescuers can transport her to hospital for its surgical detachment.

Which reminds George Irving Newett, changes changed, of his hibernating Muse—who however now bestirs herself to prompt him (better never than late?) to close this section of this Whatever with a couple of Last Things from the "Winter" of his&Ned's preadolescent boyhood. . . .

But she then on Second Thought remembers, or is by him reminded, that we *did* that already, just a few pages back. . . .

And so on Third Thought we say, "Literal and figurative First Winter, *adieu*," and bid the Reader (if he/she's still out there) to follow Pete Seeger's season-song's advice:

"*Turn, turn, turn . . .* "

spring

3

Spring has sprung. The grass has riz.
*I wonder where the flowers is?**

TO HIS PAL George Newett, "Solstices are mine," Ned Prosper declared one late-March morning back in their Stratford High days (he having been born on one, Q.E.D.). And by the same reasoning, "Equinoxes are yours."

Sixty years later, recollective G.I.N. assumes this declaration to have been made Nedward-style, his friend's right fist clenched thumb-up for emphasis, and followed some while after by "On *second* thought [forefinger raised beside thumb and pointed Georgeward like a cocked pistol], I guess that gives me just the *winter* solstice and you the *fall* equinox, right? And so

---

* "I wonder where the *birdies* is" in the anonymous original, but O.F.F. G.I.N. misremembered it as "flowers" until too late, when flowers had blossomed in the pages to follow.

on *third* thought [raising middle finger to make three, then closing thumb and fore to make the Up Yours gesture with middle
solo], *fuck* all that. Last day of winter! First of spring! Time to
lose our fucking cherries, man!"

"The word that won the war," British soldiers called that
all-purpose Anglo-Saxon expletive,** so common in adult fiction and film dialogue nowadays as to raise scarcely an eye-
brow*** (G. writes these lines on Just Another Workday
Morning in 2008), but still such a No-No back then as to make
Stratford/Bridgetown teenage boys feel macho/horny just saying it aloud. Even a dozen years later, when America's war-
after-*that* will have ended in Korea (and Ned's life as well, in
Baja California, with his first and only "novel" just begun)
and G.I.N.'s own maiden effort will have lucked into modest, short-lived print, the Word remained so touchy that the
book's university-press publisher considered it daring for one
of G.'s characters, an aggrieved wife, to demand of her former college roommate, "Why in God's name did you fuck my
husband, Jane?" To which her ex-best friend replies with a
shrug, "Takes two to tango, Barb: Go ask Pete why he fucked
me." And in the novel's even shorter-lived British edition, that

---

** I.e., the Second World War of the twentieth century's first half, won by the
Allies in Europe officially on "V-E Day" (May 7, 1945) and in the Pacific four
months later on "V-J Day" (September 2), at an estimated cost of 45,000,000
human lives.

*** E.g., the paradigmatic line in Zadie Smith's 2000 novel *White Teeth*—
"Fuck you, you fucking fuck"—which deploys it serially as verb, adjective,
and noun.

once-war-winning verb was unaccountably softened, without authorial permission, to "bed."

"And why the F-blank-blank-blank are you telling Dear Reader this?" inquires Poet/Professor/Critic/Wife Amanda Todd of *her* (still-effing-faithful and faithfully-effing) spouse. Who happens to be wondering the same thing, sort of, but suspects it may be his vagrant Muse's lead-in to Dream/Vision/Transport/ Whatever #2, which occurred not quite *on* the '08 vernal equinox, but closer thereto than #1 to the '07 winter solstice. It was, he'll grant, less a flat-out vision than a dream-inspired reverie, involving (he just now notes) not the several B's of that bad-boy Brinsley/Burlesque/Brassiere poem, but about as many S's: Springtime. Sex. Sudden Storms . . .

"In short," Mandy will tease when he bores her with all this during a pre-coital wake-up chat in each other's arms the morning after the Dream, "Much B.S. About Nothing?" But then—parodying The Isley Brothers this time instead of the Bard—she'll croon, "*C'mon, baby, lemme shake your spear!*"

Bear in mind, s.v.p., that "all this season/vision shit," as G. himself will come to call it—the pattern of more-or-less-coincident season-turns and more-or-less illuminations— hadn't yet been established. But Narrator's preoccupation with equinoxes/solstices/seasons and their association with youthful buddy Ned Prosper very much *had* been; enough so that as winter faded and spring arrived but nothing quite came together at His still-unfamiliar new workspace (the way he could imagine it might have done back in His dear "old" one in Heron Bay Estates before its tornadoing), he could not help wondering "where the flowers is." Town and campus were a-bloom with crocuses, forsythia, daffodils, jonquils, hyacinths, and tulips, but his Muse's garden-plot, while not altogether bud- and sprout-free, remained blossomless. Mocking the deep-Southern accent of one of his favorite professor-coaches back at Tidewater State U. (who often exaggerated it himself to humorous effect), G.I.N. used to advise his own StratColl coachees, "Y'all wannabe *Cree*-ay-tive Rotters, y'gotta learn how to Rot Cree-*ay*-tively." By which was meant that they should turn, re-turn, and monitor the fermenting compost of their imagination—its lumps and shards of observation, sensation, experience, and reflection as registered in notebook-notes or pungent memory—until certain of them somehow came together, germinated, and flowered into poem or story.

Creative Rotting.

On the locally-mild winter's closing day, for example, George Irving Newett's notebook noted: *Th 3/20/08: V. Equinox (= "V.E. Day"?) + 5th anniversary of U.S. Iraq invasion. New prisoner abuses revealed @ Abu Ghraib & Guantanamo. 200 anti-war demonstrators arrested in D.C. (Bush/Cheney dismiss protests). China arrests 4000 Tibetan protesters (embarrass-ment to upcoming Beijing Olympics).*

SPRING.

I wonder where Miz Muse's flowers is?

The days immediately following had their own, similarly So What? entries, each concluding with that same folk-proverbial question, to which the diarist found his fancy more and more turning, turning, turning. . . .

Wait: How's that? "Turn, turn, turn": the refrain of Pete Seeger's earlier-cited "To Everything There Is a Season," which now (i.e., "then," back in winter/spring season-turning time) reminded our floundering fictor of that anti-war folk-ballad composed by the same gifted hand after his McCarthy-era indictment by the House Un-American Activities Committee in 1956, and popular right through the Vietnam-War '60s and '70s: not the rustic "I wonder where the flowers is?", it occurred to him on one of those post-equinoctial mornings, but "Where Have All the Flowers Gone?", its poignantly circular lament here abridged as in G.I.N.'s immediate notebook-note:

> *Where have all the flowers gone?*
> *Girls have picked them every one.*
> *When will they ever learn?*
>
> *Where have all the young girls gone?*
> *Taken husbands every one.*
> *When will they ever learn?*
>
> *Where have all the young men gone?*
> *Gone for soldiers every one.*
> *When will they ever learn?*

john barth

Where have all the soldiers gone?
Gone to graveyards every one.
When will they ever learn?

Where have all the graveyards gone?
Covered with flowers every one.
When will we ever learn?
When will we ever learn? *

No time soon, it would appear. Half a century after those verses' composition, the nation remained mired in two more indecisive wars at a cost of billions of dollars per month and more than 4,000 U.S. military personnel "gone to graveyards every one," along with 100,000 Iraqis and Afghans. The economy was in deep shit from home-mortgage foreclosures, the virtual collapse of the real-estate market, the soaring cost of oil, and record federal-budget deficits. Our international approval rating sank along with the lame-duck president's, while his administration blithely continued such Fuck-the-Constitution policies as detainee torture, arrogation of power to the executive branch, and presidential "signing orders" to avoid implementing congressionally-passed bills that the White House disapproved of but chose not to veto. And the economic disparity between the wealthiest Americans and the rest of their countrymen grew to Gilded Age, brink-of-Depression size. When would we ever learn?

---

* Copyright 1961 (renewed) Fall River Music.

Maybe by the upcoming November election—but it was late March still, and G. I. Newett had no more idea than did his drowsing Muse why the F-blank-blank-blank he was telling his notebook all this. What he knew—*all* he knew, in this department—was that at bedtime on or about Sunday, March 23 (Easter Sunday, as it irrelevantly happens), as he and his mate turned to each other for their customary lights-out embrace, the "Cree-ay-tive Rotting" part of his Imagination felt the equivalent of an impending . . . orgasm? Or burp? Sneeze? Fart? He even pressed his eyes more tightly shut; squeezed his Fancy, so to speak (as unobtrusively as possible, not to alarm his bedmate), to Make It Happen. But succeeded only in falling asleep, as he realized with initial disappointment some two hours later, at First Urination Time, then again with a groggy sigh three hours after that, at Second U.T., and finally towards dawn, with the opposite of disappointment, when a brief early-spring thundershower—quite unusual for that still-chilly time of year—rolled over Stratford/Bridgetown and roused him from that long-since-signaled

DREAM/VISION/TRANSPORT/WHATEVER #2:
Spring Break Flashbang

over in a flash/bang, appropriately, of *Donner und Blitzen* *:

---

* Since lightning precedes thunder both in waking Nature and in G.I.N.'s dream, why does the German expression traditionally put the cart before the horse, as it were, or Santa's reindeer in the wrong order?

Whoosh of wind and rush of rain. "Here it comes!" *Observer/
Narrator huddles for shelter on wet beach with high-spirited
others among pilings under ocean boardwalk or pier as sudden squall moves ashore from open water.* "Coming . . . coming . . ." *Beach umbrellas cartwheel off; roaring wind blows
rain almost horizontal.* "CAME!" *Flashbang! Then going . . .
going . . .*

Gone, and the dreamer woke both exhilarated and a bit embarrassed as the brief present storm rumbled off eastward.
Embarrassed to find that he'd had a "wet dream" in both senses,
the drenching rain plus a lusty ejaculation—literal in the dream,
but virtual in waking fact, Dreamer not having experienced a
literal "nocturnal emission" since his latter teens. Embarrassed
further that the (hind-to) dream-ejaculatee had been not his beloved Amanda (whom he woke to find himself embracing from
behind, his pajama-bottomless front pressed against her ditto
rear), but . . .

    Spring Break Flashbang

*Aiyiyi: Naples, Florida, late March/early April 1952. Senior-
year spring break time for G.I.N., his Tidewater State classmate
and all-but-official fiancée Marsha Green, his still-best-buddy
Ned Prosper, and Ned's Stratford College classmate and latest girlfriend Ginny Hyman. Long-since-devirginated Virginia,
Virginia the Vagina, hymenless Hyman—oyoyoy!*

"Something bothering you?" wonders Narrator's waking wife. With whom, once he gets it duly notebooked for his Muse's consideration, he'll share a discreetly edited account of that flashbang "vision's" reverberations—immediately clear to him, unlike his earlier fire-watchtower one:

Korean War cease-fire talks in "progress," but bloody fighting rages on (armistice won't be declared for another year), as does U.S. military draft in Harry Truman's final presidential year, Narrator's and Marsha Green's last undergraduate semester at TSU, and Ned Prosper's and Ginny Hyman's at StratColl (already thus abbreviated in those pre-Internet days). Both young men have thus far avoided military conscription—as we would not have chosen to do, we believe, in World War Two—first via student deferments and then, when Selective Service Director General Hershey raised the bar, by joining our local National Guard units for weekly armory-drills, a brief summer encampment, and potential call-up to active duty should the situation worsen. As it presently seems not to be about to, but who knows? Especially since America's involvement with the weakening French government in Vietnam appears to be turning into a possible next anticommunist front, and campus rumor has it that soon only married students—maybe even only married students with children!—will continue to be draft-exempt.

"Used to be," Ned liked to say, "every fucking generation had to have its fucking war. French and Indian War! Revolutionary War! War of 1812! Civil War! Spanish-American

War! World Wars One and Two! Now it's one every goddamn
Olympiad: Cold War, Korean War, and next it'll be Vietnam or
Red China! Get us outta here!"

To Canada, maybe? We've considered that, not very seri-
ously, as a possible last resort if push actually comes to shove,
but meanwhile have our hands full deciding what to do next
fall if, as we hope, our Guard units aren't activated and our
draft-exempt status remains valid. Both of us are convinced by
now that our vocation is "Creative Rotting," and both have
applied to Master of Arts programs in that field (newly popular
in American universities) for further practice and mentoring.
Ned, who has published a short story already in The Stratford
Review *and is beginning a novel, has early-acceptance notices*
from the University of Iowa's pioneering two-year M.F.A.
program and Johns Hopkins' newer but also well-rated one-
year M.A. program. Narrator (nothing published yet, but sev-
eral pieces going the rounds of little magazines) has applied
to those and others as well, but has thus far heard positively
only from TSU's own brand-new Master's program, to be in-
augurated next fall. Our current inclination, we guess—"First
Thought," as it were—is to marry our girlfriends if necessary
to beat the draft (G. and Marsha, while not officially engaged,
have pretty much decided they'll marry anyhow, either after
college or after grad school; Ned and Ginny's connection is
more off-and-on, in several respects), put in a couple years' ad-
vanced apprenticeship somewhere or other, hope to score with
a few lit-mags or maybe even a book publisher, and consider

teaching to pay the rent, at least until and unless we "make it" as professional fictioneers.

Teaching what? How to be professional amateurs like our own coaches at StratColl and TSU—who, though pretty damn good teachers, are only occasionally publishing writers and/or scholars? Or perhaps some genuine academic discipline, in which we'll take a bona fide Ph.D. if we find one that really speaks to us? But that would mean setting aside "Creative Rotting" to research and write a scholarly dissertation. . . .

We'll cross that bridge when we come to it, after debating the subject spiritedly en route. Meanwhile . . . spring break! Having long since "lost our cherries" per Ned's first-day-of-spring Third Thought back in Stratford High—G. in his freshman college year, to the same Marsha Green with whom he has pretty much "gone steady" ever since; Ned a bit earlier, to his high school senior-prom date on, in fact, that event's occasion (not the girl's "first time," she'd confessed with some embarrassment in the rear seat of Ned's parents' car, though she was no Ginny Hyman)—we're currently "shacking up" with our girlfriends in off-campus "married student housing" apartments developed originally for WWII vets attending college on the G.I. Bill, but occasionally taken over by younger unwed couples experimenting with "sexual liberation." George and Marsha's is a Murphy-bedded studio apartment in TSU's teeming College Park area, comfortably distanced from Narrator's mildly disapproving parents, who anyhow never leave the Eastern Shore (Mom's health is failing; Dad, retired, has grown

*ever more retiring) and Marsha's more shrug-shouldered ones
up in Baltimore. Ned's and Ginny's is actually just his bedroom
in an old Victorian-style house near the StratColl campus, its
one- and two-room flats rented by an ever-shifting congeries of
married and unmarried student and non-student couples and
unattached apartment-mates. Frisky Ginny has a room and
roommate of her own in the campus dorms, but "sleeps over"
more nights than not with Ned, whose tolerant parents roll their
eyes (as much at their son's choice of partners as at his lifestyle)
but try to Understand. The two colleges' spring recesses roughly
coinciding, the foursome have decided on a Senior Spring Fling:
load some camping gear into Narrator's aging but still serviceable two-tone-green Oldsmobile station wagon and camp our
way down the coast to Key West, Florida! Southern tip of the
USA, which none of them has ever visited: Hemingway country!*

*"Sounds right nice," allows G.'s mom from the bed that
she less and less leaves (down in the Newetts' living room these
days, as she can no longer manage stairs). And Right Nice it
is, at least to begin with: high-spirited fun, laughing at one another's jokes and teasing horseplay, singing along with the car
radio, arguing Life's Big Questions, smoking pack after pack
of the new Kent filter-tip cigarettes while swigging six-packs of
beer and improvising makeshift camp-stove meals as we pup-
tent south from campground to state-park campground—not
down today's stoplight-free interstate highways, which won't be
built until the upcoming Eisenhower administration, but town-
to-town along U.S. 1 and sundry state and county roads, daily*

refilling the gas-guzzling old Olds at 25¢ per gallon through Virginia, the Carolinas, and Georgia.

"On second *thought," Narrator half-seriously complains outside Charleston, South Carolina, after the third or fourth such fill-up (his turn to pay, per the group's agreement), "maybe we should've just stuck out our fucking thumbs and hitch-hiked."*

Objects his ever-sensible Marsha, "Who'd ever pick up all four of us plus our stuff? Nobody I'd trust."

"No problem there," Ned teases: "We guys'd stand back and put you sexy types out front, one hand on your hip and the other thumb out."

Picking up the tease, "Our other thumb?" his Ginny pretends to wonder. "Not our fucking thumb, like you said before?" She examines her two thumbs, then playfully sucks at each. "Which one is that, anyhow? They taste the same to me."

"Depends on what's going on, " Ned reckons with an exaggerated wink. We're headed by then for Kiawah Island, hoping its barrier beach will be warm enough for camping, if not yet for the skinny-dip swimming that we guys, at least, look forward to down in Florida, maybe even Georgia. G. I. Newett finds Ginny Hyman's risqué antics interesting; his girlfriend does not. In the Oldsmobile's backseat he makes a show of sniffing his own thumbs, then reaches for Marsha's, but she lightly pushes his hands away. In the run-ups to their initial freshman-year intercourse, as they moved from groping through each other's clothing to groping under it, Narrator had excitedly

index-fingered the girl's moist Vulva *and anon her* Vagina *(fascinating words, their V's so evocative of the* mons Veneris *that G. always visualizes them upper-cased) before first introducing thereinto his shy but ready penis, and routinely does so still by way of foreplay and pre-coital lubrication. He has even, on occasion, lightly fingered her rectum during copulation in a sitting position or supine with Marsha on top (she objects, on hygienic more than on moral grounds, and has made clear that between them there'll be none of the anal intercourse that Ned claims to have scored now and then with Ginny. No hemorrhoids for her, thanks!). But* thumbs?

"Just a finger of speech," Ned says at that evening's camp-fire as we banter about this over beer and hot dogs. Thrusting then at Ginny's mouth a bunless frank like a toasted phallus while with his fork-free left hand feeding himself some canned baked beans right out of the cook-pot, "Fingers were invented before fucks, right?"

"Thumbs up to that," is the best Narrator can come back with, although its double entendre *isn't altogether clear to him.*

"Up to what?" Marsha pretends to want to know, and Ginny, in the spirit of the thing, makes a show of squeezing her eyes and buttocks tight while saying breathlessly, "Up to the hilt!"

Roused by such raillery, after several more beers the two couples retire, if that's the right expression, to go to it in their adjacent pup-tents, pitched amid the all but deserted because still chilly Kiawah dunes: Narrator and Marsha quietly front-to-back in the cozy dark confines of their double sleeping-bag, he withdrawing before ejaculation because they find condoms distasteful but she hasn't gotten around to being fitted for a diaphragm yet; Ned and Ginny unrestrainedly in their still lamp-lit tent as if for their neighbors' benefit: "Yes! Yes!" "How 'bout this?" "Yes!"

"Two thumbs up, d'you think?" their pleasurably-spent neighbors wonder. "Maybe big toe too?" To which Marsha adds, "That girl, I swear: She'll do anything with anybody!"

"Sounds interesting," Narrator offers experimentally, and gets no reply.

"On second thought," Ned says to G. the next day, or the day after, "to hell with getting hitched just to beat the draft." We're setting up camp on Amelia Island, just south of the Florida state line, the guys unpacking and pegging the tents while the girls take the car to a nearby general store to stock up on miscellaneous supplies, from ice and food to toilet paper and Tampax, Ginny having announced that she feels her period coming on. ("Tough titty for you guys," Narrator had teased, to which Ginny had replied, "Says who? There's more than one way to skin a cat." "And more than one cat in the bag," Ned added, "if puss comes to shove." "Shove that!" Marsha had then scolded, who'll later complain to G. that he should've done the scolding.) "You and Marsh might as well tie the knot, since that's where you seem to be headed anyhow. But I'm not ready to settle down." After seventeen straight years of school school school, he declares, kindergarten to the baccalaureate,

what he has just about decided is to attend grad school, if at all, as a Journalism major, not a Creative Rotter: a year or two of that at either Johns Hopkins or Iowa, taking his chances on the draft (Hopkins is the better university, he concedes, but its M.A. program includes only one token course in journalism, whereas Iowa offers what looks like genuine hands-on training in newspaper work), and then out of the Ivory Tower into the Arms of Life—like young Hemingway, who's been more and more on his mind as we head for the Keys.

"Experience, *man! Experience of* life, *not just books books books and talk talk talk, if we're going to have something* real *to write about."*

Yes, well: Narrator is impressed, as usual, by his friend's ideas. But he knows, and declares, that for better or worse the Arms-of-Life curriculum, especially the Hemingway-macho variety, is not for him. Marcel Proust in his cork-lined room, Franz Kafka in his workaday bureaucratic office, William Faulkner in his Mississippi campus P.O.—how Arms-of-Lifey were they, who nonetheless managed to define literary Modernism at least as much as Macho Ernie? And that other navigation-star of ours, James Joyce: How much frontline, go-where-the-action-is Experience did he require in order to move from his quietly realistic Dubliners *and* A Portrait of the Artist as a Young Man *through the complex "mythic realism" of* Ulysses *to that virtual last word in avant-garde Modernist lit,* Finnegans Wake*?*

"*That says it, right there," opines Ned as we finish setting up the tents and reward ourselves with the day's first beer:*

"After the Last Word, what comes next? Now that the Mod Squad [Narrator recalls his friend's using that term, a dozen-plus years before the debut of ABC's popular TV series thus titled] *has brought down the house, what do we Johnny-Come-Too-Latelys do with* our *turn onstage?"* Anyhow, he goes on, my redneck Willie F., as he recalls, joined the Royal Canadian Air Force in 1918, farted away the war up in Toronto, came home to lie about his combat experience in Europe, and then bummed around New York, New Orleans, and France before settling down in Ole Miss to write his masterpieces. And Joyce's "Trieste/Zurich/Paris" subscript to the Wake is a long way from Bridgetown/Stratford/College Park, n'est-ce pas?

Those are the issues most on our minds during the run-up to this spring break road-trip and en route down U.S. 1, while our girlfriends listen without much interest or speak of other things (Marsha is on track for elementary-school teacher certification; Ginny aims to be "a dietitian or something"): Just as, in the graphic arts, Impressionism was succeeded by Post-Impressionism and it in turn by Cubism, Surrealism, Abstract Expressionism, and the like, so in literature something was bound to supplant the now all-but-exhausted aesthetic of High Modernism that had defined our century thus far. In Ned's view, the torch is ready to be passed, and the questions are how best to seize it and in what new direction to run with it. By temperament less adventurous, Narrator counterargues that the whole notion of each artistic generation's need to define itself against the preceding one is a hangover from *nineteenth-century Romanticism plus a questionable analogy to scientific and technological Progress. A really new direction for our time, he half believes, might be to quit thinking in those terms and neither imitate one's immediate forebears nor define oneself against them, but, having duly surveyed the vast corpus of the "already said," simply go to one's writing-desk or typewriter, invoke one's personal muse, and see what happens, living one's life and paying the rent in whatever manner one chooses, whether as a journalist, professor, doctor, lawyer, office worker, day-laborer, or gadabout hand-to-mouth bohemian. What best suited Henry James, he likes to say, wouldn't have done for Henry Miller and vice versa, any more than Lord Byron's lifestyle would have appealed to Emily Dickinson, or Hemingway's to Kafka, but each did first-rate work of his/her kind. In short, mightn't Ezra Pound's Modernist imperative "Make it new!" (which, after all, Pound translated from Confucius!) already be getting old?* Chacun à son goût!

"What?" *wonders Ginny Hyman, our girls having returned with the goodies while their partners wrestle these Big Questions.*

"French for 'Each one limps along with his personal gout,'" *Ned assures her. Not knowing what "gout" means either, Ginny doesn't get the joke, but tells him he can French her anytime, period or no period.*

"If we-all goût each other in French," *Narrator warns,* "we'll need a circumflex. Did you pick up one of those at the store?"

"Can we please change the subject?" *Marsha suggests.*

Fifty-plus years later, "I'll second that," says Amanda Todd (among other things) upon reviewing Narrator's first-draft printout of this so-called "Flashbang." "And if a mere versifier may offer suggestions to a counter-Romantic prose fictioneer, mightn't it be advisable to give Reader some idea of what these people *look* like? What they wear, and how things feel and sound? More Sensory Texture, as we say in Cree-ay-tive Rotting One-O-One, other than the Vulval V's of your first-wife-to-be's Venusian delta?"

To which Narrator can reply only that her criticism goes without saying, he having often acknowledged both to himself and to her that were he an abler hand at such basics as the Sharp Rendition of Relevant Sensory Detail, he'd be a National Book Award winner instead of a mere Old Fart Fictionist. *Chacun à son faute*, pardon Narrator's French. . . .

"We were just four skinny middle-class Caucasian-American twenty-somethings, all of us pretty bright and none particularly wise; the girls quite attractive and the guys not bad-looking, Ned especially. All four of us light-brown-haired: Ned's and mine cut short, Marsha's and Ginny's probably ponytailed. Exact eye colors forgotten—including Narrator's own, until he checks a mirror. Marsha and I both bespectacled, mine the Dave Brubeck heavy-black-framed kind back then. Jeans and shorts and tees, and that's enough of that. Speaking of Venusian deltas, how come Anaïs Nin calls pussy 'the Delta of Venus,' when the Greek letter has its apex on top? Is the goddess standing on her head, or is Mars sixty-nining her? That's the sort of relevant sensory detail that Ned and I wrestled with back at spring break time, along with what ought to follow High Modernism in the literary arts and the A.B. in our C.V."

"Wrestle on," sighed patient Amanda Todd, and withdrew to her own Muse, as did her spouse to this slow-motion "Flashbang," wherein

Next morning, as we break camp on Amelia Island and reload the station wagon, your nerdy Narrator, who's been looking at their Florida road map, wonders aloud whether all hands are aware that the town name Naples, *on the west coasts of both Italy and Florida, is derived from* Neopolis, *which is Greek for "New Town."*

"You don't say," says Marsha, probably with a trademark eye-roll not unlike Amanda's half a century later. Ned re-declares his intention to see the real Napoli ASAP, along with "Trieste/Zurich/Paris" and the rest—and decides on the spot that in the meanwhile, instead of continuing straight down Florida's Atlantic coast to the Keys as planned, we should detour across to the Gulf Coast and have a look at that newer Neopolis down below Tampa and Fort Myers, it being reportedly a jim-dandy beach-out place, and then follow the Tamiami Trail from Naples across the Everglades to Miami and points south. Skinny-dip in the Gulf of Mexico, the Atlantic Ocean, and the Florida Straits!

"Yeah, right," says Ginny, "with my Tampax-string hanging out to turn all the guys on."

"*Worth a try*," *says Narrator, who Reader may have noticed has been being a bit flirtatious with his friend's girlfriend. His own Marsha, at least, has noticed; enough to ask him—in a private moment during their lunch-stop somewhere near Ocala, while Ned and Ginny are using the diner's washrooms—what's going on. Has her virtual fiancé got the hots for Hot-Pants Hyman?*

Yes and no, actually, he realizes and will try to explain to her once he works it out for himself en route from Ocala down past Tampa, Sarasota, and Fort Myers to Naples, still a modest little beach-town back then. He loves, respects, and intends to wed Marsha Green, whom he feels lucky to be loved by in return. For Virginia Hyman he feels neither love nor much respect—nor does Ned, he bets—but she's undeniably lively, cute, and sexy, and he'll admit to finding her flirty/frisky frankness sort of fun. . . .

Though not herself a word-player like Ned and Narrator, Marsha will be sharp enough to complain, "All those F's make it effing clear what's on my fickle fiancé's mind."

As anticipated, Narrator then finds himself explaining—to himself, to Marsha, and to Ned at the first opportunity—that while in principle he believes in sexual fidelity not only in marriage but in any committed love relationship, he can't help feeling uncomfortable both as a man and as an aspiring writer at having had no real sexual experience other than with the woman he intends to wed and be faithful to. He's no Lothario, nor does he aspire to be; no rakehell Henry Miller nor even much of an Into-the-Arms-of-Life (and other women) type like Papa Hemingway and Pal Ned. But for his dear One-and-Only to be literally his life-story's Only One is rather like . . .

"Like Faulkner trying to imagine his Yoknapatawpha without having ventured beyond it," Ned will suggest, "or Twain doing Tom and Huck without ever having left Missouri. Or Yours Truly Ned Prosper writing the Great Bridgetown/ Stratford/Seasons/Third Thought Novel without wetting his pecker in the Gulf of Mexico and plenty of other places. Gotta get ourselves some Capital-P Perspective, man!"

Our girlfriends happening to be in conversation of their own farther down Naples Beach—where we've arrived, parked the Olds near that resort-town's trademark fishing pier, and are scouting a place either to set up our tents or at least to maybe beach out overnight in our sleeping bags—Narrator grants his comrade's point, remarking however that he can't imagine Marsha's going along with it, and wondering aloud "What's this third thought/seasons stuff?" which he's never before heard mentioned in connection with Ned's novel-in-the-works.

With a smile his friend replies, "Too early to tell; still working it out. But on that other subject I've had a little talk with Generous Ginny, who for some reason or other thinks you're a pretty hot number. And she's having a little talk with your thus-far one and only, who might turn out to be a cooler chick than we've given her credit for being. Let's just see."

Greatly surprised and not a little curious, ought Narrator to have been indignant as well? No doubt. But we-all were by then several drinks into our neo-Neapolitan visit and stripped to our swimsuits in the already summer-feeling south Florida sunshine, in keeping with which we'd switched from our customary beer to more tropically appropriate dark rum and Coca-Cola. What's more, in conversation just the night before with other spring-break campers up on nearby Sanibel Island, Ned and Ginny had contrived to purchase some actual marijuana cigarettes: "reefers," which people like ourselves in the early 1950s were not unaware of, but still associated with black jazz musicians and urban street-types, although we understood the weed's popularity to be spreading. The idea had been to save our experimental stash for Key West, the intended turnaround point of our expedition—but "Qué será será," as the Doris Day hit song will have it four years later.

Half a century and more after the spring break here Flashbanged "by George I. Newett"—while Cyclone Nargis devastates Myanmar, and Senators Hillary Clinton and Barack Obama *still* go at it in the Democratic primaries for nomination as either the first female or the first African-American U.S. president—any college kids reckless enough to try skinny-dipping off the crowded beaches of bustling southwest Florida while both half stoned and half drunk would likely find themselves nailed pronto with an assortment of more or less serious charges, from Indecent Exposure to Possession of Controlled Substances. But in late March 1952, with only a scattered handful of blankets and beach umbrellas near the elevated Naples Pier and nearly

nobody in sight just a couple hundred yards down-beach, where
this frolicking foursome had staked out, "Better get our butts
wet again while we can," declared Narrator at about four that
afternoon: "Looks to me like we've got weather coming." For
indeed, although the afternoon sun remained bright and warm
as it descended over the Gulf—toward Mexico!—a dark cloud-
mass appeared to be moving their way from the south.

*Says Ned Prosper, "I'll second that," and rising unsteadily,
draws Ginny Hyman to her feet. Once up, however, she shakes
free of him, looks conspiratorially down at Marsha Green, and
says, "Butts and boobs wet, yes; bathing suits, no. You with
me, Marsh?"*

*"You bet." And to the very considerable surprise of their
male companions, by some apparent prior agreement the two
girls peel off and toss onto the blanket their swimsuit tops,
then wiggle out of the bottoms (neither item particularly scanty
by later standards: The "bikini," though invented in France
in the mid-1940s and named for the South Pacific test-site
of U.S. atomic bombs, won't become popular stateside until
after Brigitte Bardot's 1957 film* And God Created Woman
*and Brian Hyland's 1960 pop song "Itsy Bitsy Teenie Weenie
Yellow Polka Dot Bikini"—by when mere A-bombs will have
been supplanted by H-), and stagger laughing and naked together hand in hand into the all but surfless water.*

*"Well, now: Wow!" marvels Narrator at the sight of their
equally fetching forms, one of whose dainties are of course well*

known to him, the other's more interesting because here dis-played for the first time. "What an eyeful!"

"Never mind the eyeful; let's go grab us a handful," Ned proposes. "Gather some rosebuds while we fucking may."

Not at all certain what if anything is afoot, but much relish-ing the novel experiences of being "high" on "grass" and bath-ing naked à quatre, *Narrator dutifully shucks his swim trunks as Ned has done, and with him makes his wobbly way water-ward, sneaking a glance en route to confirm that his flaccid, foreskinned penis does not compare unfavorably in size to the present state of his companion's (the generation of American WASP males just then being born—the "Doctor Spock baby-boom boys"—will be the first to be routinely circumcised for hygienic reasons, as the sons of Ned Prosper and George Newett would have been if the former had lived to sire children and the latter been fertile). Already chin-deep in the chilly water, the near-hysterical girls splash each other and their approaching beaux until we four are one tumbling tangle of wet limbs and dripping hair, laughing and groping, hugging and squealing and scolding. Against which fine firm butt-cleft does that afore-cited foreskin feel itself briefly pressed? Who briefly but literally has Narrator by the balls? And who cares?*

Only the first visible lightning and audible thunder bring us ashore, still holding one another for sport and support as we stumble merrily across the shell-strewn strand to our side-by-side blankets, hurry our still-wet forms back into swimsuits (Does giggling Ginny really have a tampon-string dangling down there? Fumbling dizzily with his mist-sprayed specs, Narrator can't quite see), gather up our stuff, and hurry as best we can through rising wind up the now all but deserted beach to take shelter under the pier until the brief but violent thunder-squall passes, the raucous four of us huddled on one blanket and wrapped together in the other while lightning-bolts explode all around.

FLASHBANG!

The storm moved quickly up-shore and dissipated; the sun re-emerged in time to sink into the Gulf even more spectacularly than it had into the Chesapeake back in that Solstitial Illumination of George Irving Newett's Post-Equinoctial Vision #1—but this slow-motion "Flashbang" account of his Dream/Vision/Transport/Whatever #2 is not yet done.

"Maybe spare us the specifics?" Amanda Todd will suggest in the twenty-first century. "'The Devil's in the details,' as the saying goes."

Agreed, love—but the devilish details don't go without saying. Granted, any B-plus sophomore Creative Rotter could predict what's about to happen, more or less. . . .

"I.e., that these early-twentyish WASP-American college seniors experimenting with dope and Sexual Liberation back in mid-century are about to cross some line that will provoke a consequential Flashbang blow-up in their interpersonal relations, yes?"

Yes and no, in fact: *Yes* to the first part of that prediction; *No* to the second, where our Flashbang will presently peter out with a whimper.

"Oyoyoy, on with it, then: Peter in, peter out, and Devil take the hindmost."

That just about sums it up, actually:

To set up camp for the night, we first go back to the station wagon (but by no means go "on the wagon"; in fact, along with the pup-tents we retrieve from the back of the Oldsmobile a bottle of Gilbey's gin and another of tonic-water to supplement our all-but-done-with rum and Coke) and then trudge down to a still-undeveloped stretch of the twilit beach. Ned and Narrator pitch the tents on the storm-wet sand; the girls, still murmuring among themselves in what sounds sometimes like teasing, sometimes like arguing, cobble up from our sorely depleted larder some sort of rudimentary sandwich supper, which we wash down by Coleman lantern-light with world-temperature gin-and-tonics. Then, in lieu of dessert, we smoke the last of the marijuana, which was meant to be saved for Key West, but what the hell.

"What the hell indeed?" wonders Marsha Green, aloud. "Just what the hell do we-all think we're up to, anyhow?"

"Up to our necks in eating, drinking, and being merry?" is Narrator's guess. "For tomorrow we become Responsible Adults, or next week latest?"

"*And then* poof! *We're dead,*" *says Ned,* "*having hardly had a taste of Capital-L Life. Never mind Naples Flori-duh: Gotta see the* real *Napoli, Venezia, Pa-ree! Gotta see Tahiti, the Pyramids, the Great fucking Wall of China!*"

"*Me,*" *says Marsha,* "*I'm so effing stoned I can hardly see my effing hand in front of my face. Are we crazy, or what?*"

"Crazy 'bout you, babe," *sings Ned, and makes bold to shift herward from beside Ginny, kiss her tousled hair, embrace and collapse with her onto the blanket, laughing and spilling their drinks.*

"*What's sauce for the goose is sauce for the gander,*" *then declares Ginny,* "*and vice versa, right?*" *Rising to stand un-steadily before Narrator, she touches the bottle of Gilbey's first to his cheek, then in turn to her cleavage and her crotch, chant-ing* "G.I.N.-gin-Ginny, Ginny-gin-Gin! Let's put some hair on your chinny-chin chin!"—*a tease, Narrator will learn later, con-cocted for her somewhile earlier by Ned, along with,* "Speaking of ganders, Georgie-Porgie, why not take a real gander at what you've been sneaking peeks at all afternoon?"

Nuzzling his neck, she takes his arm as if to lead him tent-ward. As he pulls himself up, "What the fuck, guys?" *Narrator wonders, seeing Ned and Marsha, still loosely embraced, grin-ning up at him from their blanket.*

Says Ned with a shrug, "Arms-o'-Life, man: Nothing ven-tured, nothing gained." *Marsha—Narrator's own Marsha!—squeezes shut her eyes and lips and gives the merest nod of as-sent, as if to say (what in fact she'll say later, in past tense),* "It's

*what you've obviously been wanting to do, so go do it and be
done with it."*

We do.

"So we're done with it, right? I mean with this whole Flashbang-
whatever, and now we can both get back to work and on with
our lives?"

We'll get there, dear Mandy, after one or two devilish details. Your quote-Narrator-unquote was initiated that night
into the guilty pleasures not only of "infidelity" (if that term
applies to what seems to have been both consented to and re-
ciprocated by all parties concerned, none of them married and
only one couple more or less pledged), but to anal intercourse
as well, at Ms. Hyman's direction, she being by then in full
menstrual flow, reluctant to bloody up the bedding but not at
all to take it up the ass, which (she assured her much-impressed
partner-*du-soir*) she and Ned sometimes did for sport even
when she wasn't Tampaxed. A little Vaseline (which she just
happened to have in her pack), a full firm erection (which her
aroused tutee happened to have in hand), and Bingo (no contraceptive measures necessary)! 'Twas an experience not to be
repeated in George Irving Newett's *curriculum vitae* thus far,
nor likely to be at this late stage thereof. Although not prudes,
neither Marsha Green, to whom he will be happily married for
three years and then regrettably ever less so for two more, nor
Amanda Todd, with whom he remains happily, totally, faith-
fully bonded after four decades, was/is inclined to butt-fucking.

As Mandy put it pithily when her then-still-frisky spouse suggested same during one early "period" in their marriage, "*A*,
it hurts (been there, done that). *B*, it's shall-we-say unsanitary.
And *C*, it can lead to hemorrhoids. You want to get your rocks
off when I've got the rag on, we'll think of something."

End of quote, and of erotic/scatologic specificity.

*"Satisfied?" Marsha wants to know later that night, after
the men have returned, quite spent, to their usual tent-mates.
Narrator is tempted to reply, "On the whole, yes," but resists
the poor pun and says instead, "I guess. You?"*

*"Don't ask," orders his soon-to-be-bride, cuddled sleepily
now against him in the tented dark. "And no more of this Arms-
of-Life stuff for us, okay? It's each other's arms or none. Or else."*

"Agreed," Narrator assures her, and himself.

*Over next morning's breakfast and camp-breaking, the
four of us shake our heads at having been simultaneously
so stoned and boozed, but avoid the subject of our partner-
swapping. Impish Ginny, however, manages to make a little*
mwah *at Narrator over our instant coffee, and Ned, when the
girls aren't looking, tilts his head toward Marsha and gives
Narrator a knowing wink and nod of approval.*

*We presently repack and trudge carward with our stuff.
There seems to be, along with the subtropical humidity, some
small voltage in the air, but Narrator, for one, is still too hung
over to assess it. Setting down his load at the station wagon's*

tailgate, he fishes in the side pockets of his Bermuda shorts, wondering aloud, "Where'd the fucking keys get to?" and then locates them in one of the buttoned front pockets, where he'd secured them along with his Swiss Army knife against getting accidentally dropped in the sand and lost. Without our customary josh and banter, we open and make to reload the old Olds, Narrator beginning vaguely to wonder what if anything is afoot. Then "Y'know what?" Ned Prosper asks or declares, standing at the open tailgate with his spread fingertips contemplatively tented together: "On third *thought, I say fuck the fucking Keys: Let's haul our asses home."*

"Home?" cries disappointed Ginny. "Who wants to go there?"

But "I'm for it," promptly seconds Marsha: "No more of this weirdo crap for me."

In the log of this aborted odyssey that he's been keeping for possible literary use down the road and will draw upon in the century to come for this reconstruction, George Irving Newett cannot resist noting en route back north that although they failed to reach the continental USA's southernmost point, he at least attained Ginny Hyman's. At the time, however—also disappointed, but sensing that Ned's and Marsha's minds are made up—what he says is, "So it's hasta la vista, *Hemingwayville? Farewell to Arms-of-Life?"*

"Nope," replies Ned, who's at the wheel both literally and figuratively. "Just end of this rough-draft chapter."

From the rear seat, where she and Narrator are wearily but determinedly holding hands, Marsha agrees: "We need a break from spring breaking, is what we need."

"Shucks," laments Ginny, but then half-turns in her passenger seat to wink at all hands. "Well: At least this Rough-Draft Chapter ended with a bang, *right?"*

But not its Flashbang retelling, which closes with neither bang nor whimper—just quietly. Back in Maryland after two marathon driving-days and nights, the foursome split up to end the spring recess with their separate families before returning to Stratford College and Tidewater State University.

"Last night of spring break before last half-semester before graduation," Ned Prosper observed over his and George Newett's final National Bohemian beer of that evening in the Prospers' club basement, where the pair had been reviewing the ups and downs of their aborted odyssey.

"You and your Last Things," G. imagines he replied.

"Yup. Like, think of that Naples shit as your last fling at bachelorhood before you take your bachelor's degree and marry Marsha till death do you part. Or divorce, whichever cometh first." For the couple had indeed resolved en route home, partly in reaction to "that Naples shit," to tie the knot promptly after Commencement Day in as simple a ceremony as possible, with Ned as Best Man and Marsha's kid sister as Maid of Honor. After which—and maybe a weekend honeymoon at nearby Ocean City or Rehoboth Beach—bride and groom would take whatever summer jobs they could find before starting their M.F.A. and M.Ed. studies at TSU in September.

"You?"

"Me." He sipped and swallowed; shook his head. "Me, I'm outta here, man: Neither Arms-of-Marriage nor Arms-of-Academe for this here Cree-ay-tive Rotter." Ginny Hyman, he assumed we would agree, was a good sport and frisky in bed, but no more ready to be any man's wife than was he to be any woman's husband. (He trusted, by the way, that that little pup-tent experiment in partner-swapping had put no lasting strain on the Newett/Green connection: "Marsha did it for *your* sake, you know, hoping it'll scratch that particular itch of yours for keeps.") As for grad school, they'd been over that already: If G. thought it the Best Next Thing for his Muse, then more power to him—and to that Muse, whom Ned imagined as a Marsha/wifey type. But his own was more a flirty-fickle, catch-me-if-you-can, anything-goes sort of chick, as changeable as wind, weather, or Ginny Hyman. If he was ever to complete his novel-in-the-works (which, unlike all previous manuscripts, he had steadfastly declined to share or even really discuss with his longtime Bridgetown buddy, still claiming it to be in too early gestation even to risk talking about), he and She would have to do it *à deux*. He intended to work at it as much as possible for the remainder of his final college semester; then, along with academic commencement, he would graduate from StratColl's Reserve Officer Training Corps (to which he'd switched from the National Guard in his junior year) into the

Army's Language School out in California to pick up an Asian
tongue or two—thence to Korea or wherever the Action was,
but safely behind the lines rather than in a hellish foxhole on
Hill Number Whatever.

G., who'd more or less seen this coming, shook his head. "I
wish you luck, man."

"Me too, and you too—with our fucking muses and
elsewise."

That evening—the last with his longtime friend that George
Irving Newett can clearly reimagine—ended with the pair of
them recollecting together an incidental but still-vivid scene
from their high school graduation days (it would resurface sub-
sequently in G.I.N.'s mostly-unpublished fictive efforts and,
he'd bet, in the lost manuscript of Edward "Ned" Prosper's
Seasons-or-whatever novel as well):

On a hot, humid, mid-to-late-June afternoon in 1948
(Ned, being Ned, recalled it as Last Day of Spring), the pair
are stretched out on that mud/sand "beach" near Stratford's
Matahannock River bridge, reviewing yet again the StratColl
and TSU course-catalogues in search of a major more specific
and to their taste than General Arts & Sciences while also idly
watching a clutch of their fellows diving into the river from a
high platform that the town recently added to the (newly improved) waterfront park in hopes of discouraging use of the
highway bridge itself as a launch pad. Art History. Botany.
Chemistry. French. Geology. Literature. Philosophy. Physics.
Psychology. Zoology. Such a smorgasbord of ways to spend

one's working life, one's mortal prime time! And there exactly, they agree, is the rub: If one had fifty lives to live, or even the modest feline nine, one could do *A* for a career *this* time, try *B* next, then *C* and *D* or *G* and *H* or even *A* again, reliving and improving upon one's prior go at it. But with only a single measly ride on the carousel, how to choose among Horse and Lion, Rhinoceros and Giraffe, as one's mount for the too-quick spin?

Out on the platform, meanwhile, some do the swan, some the backflip, some the cannonball, some the unintended, ignominious, and painful bellyflop. In every case, it's Climb, Dive, Whatever, Splash.

"That there is *life*," observes Ned. "Except in life we get just one dive." Both then and upon subsequent recollection, "Crock of shit," the two agree (a popular negative in that time and place): Four quick decades after college, if they're lucky, before they'll be old farts on a pension—and already at age eighteen they've spent nearly half that much time getting ready to get ready! Will they end up like the fellow they now remark out there who, when his turn comes at the springboard's tip, merely shrugs his shoulders and steps off, turns up his palms as he falls feet-first, and goes under having attempted nothing en route?

"At least he made a splash," ventures G.I.N.: "Better than sinking without a trace, like most."

"Plus he entertained us all for about two seconds; let's grant him that. But shit, man: We want to do more than just make a splash, don't we? Something *worthwhile* . . . " That last inflected *à la* his parents, who hope their son will "find his calling" in one of the do-good professions: medicine, scientific research, the law (in its less venal aspects)—perhaps even (like themselves) education?

Once again his friend envies Ned Prosper such parents. Enough for Fred and Lorraine Newett that their son will be "going off to college," the first in either of their families ever to have had that privilege. They would not presume to suggest a career major, although Dad has heard tell of something called Business Administration, and Mom agrees that that sounds Nice.

"Me," says Ned now, "I want a damn Nobel Prize—and not just 'cause it'd make me famous, but 'cause I'd be famous for doing something *worth doing*, y'know? Something *worthwhile*."

Responds much-impressed G., who could never have presumed to such lofty ambition, "Wow! O*kay!* So come on, man: I'll race you!"

"To Stockholm?" Ned pretends to wonder. "You're on, pal!"

But it's into the sea-nettled Matahannock that they run, risking a sting or two for the pleasure of a cool-off in the still spring-chilly river.

"And four years later," observed Ned Prosper four years later at the last-night-of-spring get-together that prompted the above recollection, "here we are: two wannabe Cree-ay-tive Rotters still looking for the road to Stockholm."

"Speak for yourself," advised George Irving Newett: "Me, I'm still clearing my narrative throat, trying to find my Capital-V fucking Voice."

"Likewise—though I suspect I may actually be finding it in this new *Seasons* thing I'm into. I'll let you know. *So . . .* " Last clink of near-empty bottles: "May our testicles finally descend and our throats clear, and may the better Rotter take the Prize."

He had, by the way, he then added, formulated a proper definition of our presumptive calling as pronounced by that Deep-South undergrad writing-coach of mine over at Tidewater State—a definition that G.I.N. was free to pass along to the guy at baccalaureate time: "Cree-ay-tive Rotting is, quote, *the active decomposing and digesting of life-experience and the corpus of literature, followed by their artful recomposing into new fiction and verse*, end of quote. Shall we get on with it, in the arms of our separate and different muses?"

"Good idea," declares Amanda Todd 5.6 decades later, when her husband finally winds up, for the present, his account of this Spring Break Flashbang Vision/Whatever: "And a not-bad definition of your and your pal's quote Cree-ay-tive Rotting— always bearing in mind, however, that what most often follows Decomposition and Digestion is a load of shit."

"Q.E.D.?"

"No no no. I'm enjoying this, actually: my One-and-Only's pre-Me years, composted. Quite a buddy you had there."

"That he was, love: Taught me more than just how to jerk off and make out and smoke and drink. Taught me how to swim; how to drive a car; how to go to college. Taught me to love the arts, especially Capital-L Literature, and even to have Capital-A Ambitions in that department."

"I'm grateful to him for all that, Gee. Wish I'd known him."

"Just as well you didn't, or you'd likely be in *his* pup-tent instead of mine."

All this on a late-spring evening in C.E. 2008: not the last of StratColl's spring break (by then well past, along with the academic year) nor the last of the season itself, still a few weeks from its solstitial close, but an early-June post-dinner P.M. In the course of which, appropriately, as wife and husband retired to their separate spaces for their routine hour of pre-TV-&-bedtime reading, a fast-moving thundershower rolled by to south of us, as if conjured by G.I.N.'s recollected vision. Nothing destructive, like those that had lately flooded Iowa and Indiana and broken levees along the Mississippi, not to mention the typhoon that would drown the Philippines on the approaching equinox: just a bit of wind and rain, one blink of the neighborhood lights (requiring all digital clocks to be reset, but no auxiliary power-generators to be fired up), and an appropriately impressive display of lightning well downriver from Stratford/Bridgetown, which we set aside our reading to admire together.

"Bye-bye springtime; come on summer," Mandy commented. "When, as Gee Gershwin tells us, *the livin' is easy,* even for us not-yet-retired academics." More seriously then, "Ma

Nature is obviously in synch with your and your late friend's equinox/solstice/seasons thing: Let me know what y'all come up with down the road, OK? On the shortest night of the year?"

"My midsummer night's dream?" it occurred to Narrator to wonder. "Or would that be in mid-August, since the equinox just *begins* the season? I've never been sure which."

"So go Google it, and let me know," his Ms. suggested, and returned to whatever she'd been reading.

As did Narrator to whatever *he*'d been, but found himself too distracted, even overwhelmed, by the confluence of associations—seasons/*Seasons*, timely tempests, and the prospect of an upcoming midsummer night's Dream/Vision/Whatever #3— either to read or to reboot his closed-for-the-night computer. When he does, next morning, he'll learn from Wikipedia that the European "midsummer" holiday, pre-Christian in origin, marked the ancients' "middle of summer," later the astronomical *beginning* of that season, and by coincidence the nativity of St. John the Baptist ("St. John's Day"), and is celebrated in North European countries especially by festivals, bonfires, and—in Sweden anyhow, where warm weather arrives late— by Maypole-dancing in the last week of June rather than on May Day. But by then (last week of spring: Senator Hillary Clinton has finally conceded the Democratic presidential nomination-race to Barack Obama; the price of regular gasoline in the USA has for the first time in its history topped $4 a gallon; Zimbabwean President Robert Mugabe's thugs have stalled that nation's runoff election by murdering numerous of his opponent's supporters; wildfires are blazing in northern California; and deadly Typhoon Fengshen is bearing down on the Philippines) what's really mushrooming from his imagination's compost-pile is, on First Thought anyhow, his Next Big Project: not another O.F.F.-novel, but a memorial-memoir of growing up with Ned Prosper, who if he'd lived might well have become the Capital-W Writer that George Irving Newett didn't. The "Winter" of their Bridgetown childhood and preadolescence, as suggested by Narrator's solstitial fire-tower vision, followed by the Springtime of their adolescence and vigorous young adulthood: 1944–54 for unlucky Ned; for his memoirist, 1944–59, maybe? Mid-teens to late-twenties, by when his own attempts at fiction were going the rounds in not-always-unsuccessful search of publication?

Problem: This long-since-sprung "Spring" chapter of this whatever-it-turns-out-to-be is clearly winding down, but our guys are still only at the beginning of their twenties. Seven Spring-years yet to go for G., in the course whereof he'll complete his Master of Arts degree at TSU, wed his self-designated "Mistress of Artist" Marsha Green, score an entry-level instructorship in English Composition down at Marshyhope State College on the lower Eastern Shore, manage after all to

---

* Korean-language instruction at the Army Language School in Monterey; busy spare-time sampling of assorted West Coast attractions, from Valley Girls to giant-redwood forests and chilly Pacific surfing, Existentialism to Zen Buddhism; and the ever-shape-shifting programme of his novel-in-the-works—whose title, he reported without explanation, he was changing "on Second Thought" from *Seasons* to *Every Third Thought*.

place a few short stories in those more or less obscure lit-mags, complete his first (and thus far still his only published) novel, and terminate by mutual consent (Irreconcilable Differences) that short-lived first marriage. Only two more years for his nipped-in-the-bud buddy before N.'s Arms-of-Life curriculum* leads him—evidently by meaningless, random accident—into the arms of death. Experience-rich, lesson-teaching years for both, well worth memoiring! But always at his back Narrator hears, not "Time's winged chariot hurrying near" (as in Andrew Marvell's seventeenth-century lyric pitch "To His Coy Mistress," a favorite of both of these twenty-somethings), but rather . . . some sort of *birdcall*, is it?

Pigeon? Dove? Canada Goose?

Cuckoo?

summer

Sumer is icumin in,
Lhude sing cuccu.
Groweth sed and bloweth med,
And springth the wude nu—
*Sing cuccu!**

ON A MID-JULY Maryland mid-day some three weeks past
the summer solstice, Poet/Professor/Life-Partner/Critic
Amanda Todd, having reviewed at her mate's request the foregoing chapter ("Spring") of his whatever-it-might-turn-out-to-
be, declared or announced to its author, "Two questions-slash-
comments, okay?"

"Slash away." No Vision/Transport/Whatever #3 as yet,
to George Irving Newett's perplexed disappointment. But
while he'd been awaiting its arrival, Tropical Storm Arthur

---

* Anonymous, late-thirteenth/early-fourteenth century.

and Hurricane Bertha, as if summoned by his tempest-tossed Vision #2, had kicked off in the Caribbean what looked to be another busy Atlantic hurricane season. The Dow-Jones Industrial Average had dropped from its record high of 14,000 the previous October to below 11,000 in the subsequent worldwide economic recession, and continued its alarming downward slide. And we Newett/Todds, the night before this lunch-hour conversation, had enjoyed a gorgeous full Buck Moon* and brilliant Jupiter gleaming over Stratford/Bridgetown. Now, having finished our morning's separate muse-work, we were sipping smoothies and nibbling granola-bars in the air-conditioned kitchen of our rented condominium, it being too hot and humid outside to lunch on its little screened porch.

"Well: To begin with?" Mandy began, with the interrogative rising inflection lately picked up from her students. "If I remember correctly—which I do, because I checked it?—back in your 'Winter' chapter, when your Narrator-guy steps up into StratColl's Shakespeare House to meet his missus for lunch on the December solstice, he's reminded of his trip-and-fall in *Shakespeare's* house on the September equinox, right? And *that*—plus the sight of that kid with the Jehovah's Witness *Watchtower* mag—reminds him of his fire-tower climb with Pal Neddie's family in their kiddie-days, when he first learned

---

* So named by Algonquin Indians because the male Virginia White-Tail deer's fuzzy new antler-buds begin to emerge just about then—but also called by them the Thunder Moon, for the frequency of such storms in that season.

about equinoxes and solstices—which leads to his so-called Solstitial Illumination of Post-Equinoctial Vision #1. All reasonable enough. You with me so far?"

Her husband supposes so: "I mean, I *wrote* the freaking thing. . . . "

"Then maybe you can explain what Narrator doesn't: why it is that what also jump-starts his fire-tower illumination is the kid's Everyman edition of Will's comedies. I remember how you went on about that over lunch at Bozzelli's, but I don't think you've ever said exactly what its relevance was, other than Shakespeare House/Shakespeare's house/Shakespeare's plays. Are we supposed to think of that big-deal Illumination as G.I.N.'s Mid*winter* Night's Dream, or what?"

Well, now: Author realized and readily admitted that in fact he hadn't known exactly *what* the connection was: only that it was sudden and strong. His mate's suggestion struck him as both plausible and too clever by half; now that she'd raised the question, however, its answer seemed evident, especially in retrospect from that storm-fraught Spring Break Flashbang Vision #2: The Shakespeare Connection was not *A Midsummer Night's Dream*, but that grimmer "comedy" *The Tempest*. Prosper=Prospero, the storm-conjuring wizard protagonist of that play, who predicts at its close (how had G. not seen so obvious an echo before, especially given the last working title of Ned's lost opus-in-progress and his friend's habit of naming First, Second, and Third Thoughts?) that henceforth his "every third thought shall be the grave"!

"Hiding in plain sight," supposed Amanda, to whom the connection had seemed self-evident enough not to need remarking. And Ned himself, oddly, back in their apprentice-writer days, had never, as far as G. can recall, ever linked his surname to that of Shakespeare's island-stranded Duke of Milan.

"What I *do* remember his saying early on is that if a storyteller hung a name like 'Mister Prosper' on his tale's eminently successful protagonist, we would wince at his heavy-handedness—unless the piece was a Capital-A Allegory or a flat-out farce, with supporting characters like Suzy Spendthrift and Mary Miser."

"Or," Mandy added, "unless Protagonist P. at the end of the day turned out despite his name to be a loser at everything he set his hand to, in which case he himself might gnash his teeth at *life's* ponderous irony, not the author's. Right? I remember your telling me all this forty years ago, when you and I were a hot new item."

To the tune of the Mary Hopkin recording from back then, "*Those were the da-a-ays, my friend,*" G. crooned to his still-beloved; "*we thought they'd ne-ver end.* The blooming summertime of our lives."

"So go have yourself a Capital-V Vision about it."

He'd work on it, Narrator promised. But he believed she mentioned *two* question/comments regarding his tentative draft-thus-far. What was the second?

"Well . . . " Final slurp of smoothie. "*You're* supposed to be the story-maker-upper in this condo, and me the mere lyric poet—"

"*Mere* shmeer," her husband interrupts to tut-tut.

"But I can't help thinking that something more *interesting* ought to be going on in the present time of this narrative than just a series of visions that trigger Narrator's recollections of his boyhood with Ned Prosper, and the ho-hum suspense of whether they'll add up to another G. I. Newett-book. . . . "

"Something like what?, its author wonders," its author wondered.

"Oh, you know . . . like maybe some major bump in the long happy road of Narrator's marriage, for example, to rev up the story? Suppose I confess an ongoing late affair with one of our StratColleagues, e.g., or maybe discover that you have a grown illegitimate son or daughter by some pre-Me fling of yours that you never got around to telling me about? *That* would juice things up!"

Parodying Andrew Marvell's aforecited lyric, "*Help like that I shall refuse,*" Narrator intoned, "*till the conversion of the Juice*—into Manischewitz blackberry wine, maybe, or something else non-toxic. So who'd you hump, luv? And when, and why?"

She smiled one of her Mandy-smiles and raised her smoothie-glass in salute: "See? Situation revved up; Reader hooked. *Lhude sing cuccu!*"

"Hooked?" would-be-Author protested. "By such cornball chick-lit plot IEDs* as those? But thanks for trying."

---

* Pentagon acronym for the Improvised Explosive Devices deployed by Al Qaeda and other terrorists for deadly roadside bombings. Not to be confused with the IUDs (intrauterine devices) deployed contraceptively by women of Amanda Todd's generation in their pre-menopausal years before the development and marketing of birth-control pills—unnecessary in the case of the Todd/Newetts, it will turn out to their mid-Summer disappointment. Read on.

"My pleasure—as has been the all-but-bumpless story of Us. May it remain so."

"Here's to that: No Plot-Complications or Rising Action in *our* story, s.v.p."

Click of empty glasses (no symbolism intended).

"So on with your Summer," then bade George Irving Newett's virtual muse. "And if you include this conversation in your chapter-in-progress, consider changing *cornball* chick-lit plot-hooks to *cuckoo* chick-lit et ceteras. Another wink at Dear Reader?"

"Gotcha. I think?"

Heat expands; cold contracts. Although the calendric seasons are of equal three-month length, their days get longer as winter warms into spring and spring into summer, as do the corresponding life-seasons in this narrative. The "Winter" of Ned Prosper's and George Newett's childhood was a mere dozen years, 1930–42; the "Spring" of their adolescence and young adulthood was meant to be sixteen years (1943–59, through their teens and twenties), and in G.'s case was. But the "Summer" of Narrator's full and more-or-less-robust maturity—from his thirties through his fifties, as G. sees it—1960 through 1989, let's say—is nearly twice that span. How to squeeze it into a single chapter?, he wonders to his balky Muse. And what has it to do with nipped-in-the-bud Ned, who didn't live to live it, and of whom one understood this rambling narrative to have become a memoir?

What appeared to be the case, its perpetrator realized as Common Era 2008 approached its literal midsummer (i.e., August 21, midway between June solstice and September equinox), was that nothing of Ned Prosper remained to memoirize except his end—a tale quickly told, as there's frustratingly little of it to tell:

On a mid-June Saturday in 1954 (stalemated Korean War ended by armistice dividing country at 38th Parallel into communist North and democratic South, but Senator Joseph McCarthy's red-baiting witch-hunt continues, and public-institution academics like George Irving Newett—entry-level Instructor of English Composition at Marshyhope State on Maryland's lower Eastern Shore—must grit teeth and sign loyalty oath denying past or present Communist-party membership), twenty-four-year-old Second Lieutenant Edward "Ned" Prosper, on weekend leave from the Army Language School, drove with one Ms. Lucinda Barnes, a young civilian employee in the ALS library and his girlfriend-of-the-moment, from Monterey down to Baja California in her bucktooth-bumpered cream-and-green Buick Special sedan in search of warmer-water surfing than could be found nearer by: ideally (Ms. Barnes would later report), a spot isolated enough for them to ride the waves and each other au naturel. Somewhere below Tijuana they located an adequately secluded stretch of beach and commenced what sounds like a replay of that

*earlier-narrated southwest Florida Spring Break Flashbang of
1952, but with only one couple this time, and thus no partner-
swapping. Consumption of mucho tequila and Acapulco Gold
pot while singing with mock-military zest the Latino lyrics of
La Cucaracha,* duly followed by naked woozy frisking on the
sand and in the surf, including not-very-successful attempts to
ride the waves while both liquored and stoned. Project soon
abandoned ("On Second Thought," G. imagines N. proposing) in favor of mere splashing and body-surfing in the break-
ers, and that in turn, by Ms. Barnes anyhow, for passing out on
their beach-blanket while her boyfriend carried on out there.
"Bit more of a swim," she believed she remembered his calling
after her as she staggered to shore, "and then I'll join you."*

*But he never did. No sign of him when she woke up some
while later, sunburned and hung over; nor any thereafter, despite her ever-more-frantic searching and calling up and down
the beach and adjoining headlands, then an at-least-perfunctory
search by Tijuana authorities upon the hysterical gringuita's
reporting the matter to them, and more extensive follow-up
investigations by both the U.S. military and the missing man's
grief-stricken parents, who flew out with sister Ruth from
Maryland to Mexico and then Monterey. By general best-guess
consensus, he must have been either caught in a riptide and*

---

* "*La cucaracha, la cucaracha / Ya no puede caminar. / Porque no tiene,
porque le falta / Marijuana que fumar.*" Rough gringo translation: "The cockroach, the cockroach / Can march no farther. / Because he has no, because he's
lacking / Marijuana to smoke."

carried out farther than he could swim back in his impaired condition, or attacked by a shark: Both perils were reported in the vicinity from time to time. A third possibility briefly considered by the military was that with or without Ms. Barnes' knowledge and collusion, Lt. Prosper had planned and staged his disappearance in order to desert the service and embrace some other of life's arms. But while it was true that in recent communications to his family and to G., as well as in conversation with his Language School comrades, he had expressed a growing boredom with his military life and a hope to move on before very long to some interesting Next Thing that would also give him more time for his writing, criminal desertion and the attendant elaborate subterfuges were altogether out of character for him. Moreover, his clothing, backpack, passport, and wallet were on the beach and in the Buick, where he'd left them, and his other belongings all in place back in his quarters. Suicide, then, perhaps? But except for the aforementioned restlessness he had seemed in fine spirits, all hands testified, and very much involved with that "Third Thought" opus-in-presumable-progress, which despite G.'s several requests his friend had steadfastly declined to share with him until at least its first draft was complete. No trace of Edward "Ned" Prosper from that mid-June afternoon to this mid-August one fifty-four summers later—nor of that manuscript (which, despite her hungover and much-distressed condition, Ms. Barnes was confident he'd not brought along with them to Mexico, much less taken into the surf).

What kind of story-ending is that?

Well: As Ned himself remarked apropos of something-or-other in the last letter G. received from him, shortly before that ill-fated south-of-the-border excursion,

> *Our lives are not stories, G-Man. The story of one's life is not one's life; it is one's Story (one of one's stories, anyhow). ¡Hasta la vista, amigo mio, and on with the story! N.*

That was that—and the unfinishedness of it, as Reader may have noticed, haunts Narrator to this hour, this minute, this sentence. Was his friend even *really* writing that "Seasons" thing through the two years between spring break '52 and June '54, or did he for some inscrutable reason only *pretend* to be absorbed in doing so while G. himself completed his modest Tidewater State M.F.A., scored his first modest short-story publications (which Ned praised—and helpfully appraised—with a perceptive astuteness unmatched by any subsequent G.-readers except Amanda Todd), and commenced his modest academic career? Could it be that that fiction so long in the works was in fact fictitious?

Aiaiai, oyoyoy—and on with *this* unended (but presumably not ending-less) story. In their ambitious early-apprentice-writer days, Ned Prosper once remarked with apparent pride to George Newett, apropos of who knows what, that his bowels moved regularly once a day, always so promptly after breakfast that he scarcely had time to brush his teeth before defecation. "That's so *anal*!" G. had been pleased to tease, both young men having duly studied Freud at their separate colleges. "Anal my ass," had responded Ned; "I just don't take any shit off my bowels, you know?" Whence he went on to declare that the same was going to apply to his Muse: If, as Thomas Edison remarked, genius is "one percent inspiration and ninety-nine percent perspiration," then the remedy for artistic *constipation* is to grunt harder. "When you're stuck, bust your gut; better a bloody stool than none."

Yuck. But applying this maxim to the stalled or anyhow idling "Summer" section of the narrative in hand, on the afore-invoked "midsummer" Delmarva morning of August 21, 2008 (Beijing Olympics in full swing; Barack Obama prepares to accept Democratic presidential nomination at upcoming party convention in Denver), its narrator, whose bowel and other movements had ever been less programmed than his late buddy's, booted up his word processor, scrolled to where he had too long since left off, and boldly typed the small-caps boldface heading

DREAM/VISION/TRANSPORT/WHATEVER #3:
Midsummer Night's Dream

Then he closed his eyes, drew and held a *very* deep breath, clenched as tight as possible his fists and every other clenchable muscle in his high-mileage but still serviceable body, and waited to see which would happen first: inspiration, perspiration, loss of consciousness, or loss of nerve. . . .

john barth

None of those, it turned out: merely the end of his capacity
for suspended animation. Literally dizzied by the unprecedented
attempt, after who knows how many seconds or (less likely)
minutes he opened eyes, resumed breathing, relaxed muscles,
woozily regarded that boldface subtitle, and by-George found
himself typing below it something that might after all serve, if
not quite for a midsummer night's dream, at least for

D/V/T/W #3:

—changing its subtitle to the date implied in his wife's reference, somewhile back, to "forty years ago, when you and I were
a hot new item." I.e.,

1968,

the height of the High Sixties, a full fourteen years after Ned
Prosper's disappearance: Pop Art, the New Feminism, Black
Power, Counterculturalism. *Hair*, the Beatles, bell-bottoms and
miniskirts, beards and bongs. Massive anti-Vietnam War demonstrations in D.C. and elsewhere; sometimes-violent student "sit-
ins" on college campuses (even at normally tranquil StratColl),
often broken up by tear-gas-firing National Guardsmen.
"Cultural Revolution" in Mao's China, Tet Offensive in Saigon,
nationwide leftist strikes in France, black urban ghettos aflame
across the USA. Martin Luther King and Robert F. Kennedy
assassinated, and Richard Nixon narrowly elected president
over Hubert Humphrey after turbulent Democratic convention
in Chicago. A transformative, near-apocalyptic year in many

parts of the world—but for us George Newetts and Amanda Todds, "the blooming summertime of our lives." G.'s five-year first marriage was by then a decade behind him: Marsha Green had successfully remarried and, one heard, was turning out children in Michigan, Minnesota, or Montana (relieved of mailing her monthly alimony checks, her ex-husband knew only that her new locale, like her former one and her first name, began with an *M*). Thirty-eight-year-old George, in his eighth year at Stratford College, had newly attained the rank of Full Professor in the college's English and Creative Writing Department on the strength of his teaching record and his modest-but-adequate publications. In his post-Marsha, post-Marshyhope years he had enjoyed a couple of semi-serious romances (fewer hookup opportunities in small-town Stratford than at Tidewater or Marshyhope State Universities, with their larger faculty, staff, and surrounding community), which however—like those multistage NASA rockets that lift off successfully but whose subsequent stages misfire or otherwise fail to place their payload into orbit—fizzled out after a semester or two. Reconciling himself, on the sexual front anyhow, to his condition of potent sterility or sterile potency, he had grown more or less resigned to bachelorhood, much as he missed the sort of loving companionship that he'd enjoyed before his marriage soured.

Then came, not 1968 yet, but the summer of '66, when StratColl's English Department, in need of a new Creative Writing hand, hired twenty-four-year-old Amanda Todd as an entry-level assistant professor: M.A. from the Johns Hopkins

Writing Seminars, where she'd also been a Graduate Teaching Assistant and was kept on for an additional year as a "Super-T.A."; a half-dozen poems published already in reputable quarterlies; well-read, sharp-minded and sharp-looking, immediately popular both with her students and with her colleagues. Then 1967, in the late October whereof, only two members of the Stratford faculty, George Newett and Amanda Todd, joined 50,000 other demonstrators in the massive anti-Vietnam War protest across the Chesapeake in Washington that would inspire Norman Mailer's *The Armies of the Night*. The pair were already by then ever-closer friends as well as mutually admiring colleagues, respectful of their separate muses and their shared departmental responsibilities; the twelve-year difference in their ages and two-notch difference in their academic titles seemed ever less significant as they'd come to know each other better over the semesters. Nothing really "romantic" between them yet as of fall '67, but their ever-more-frequent shared pleasures—lunches *à deux*; the occasional movie, concert, or student theater production; side-by-side workouts in the college gym; singles tennis as well as mixed doubles with other faculty or student couples; canoeing on the Matahannock from the college's waterfront facility—had taken on an unmistakably flirtatious air despite their mutual reserve: his lest he seem to be exploiting his seniority, hers lest she seem to be courting it. The adrenaline-rush of that October march from Capitol to Pentagon, however, with its encircled-semaphore peace icons, its multi-thousand-voice chants (*"Hey hey, LBJ: How many kids did you kill today?*") and hippie banners urging America to *MAKE LOVE, NOT WAR!* nudged them across an unacknowledged threshold. Having driven over to D.C. in G.'s Volkswagen Beetle among a caravan of Stratford-student cars, when they rejoined the exhausted group for the less coordinated return trip Professor Newett found himself announcing to them that he and Professor Todd would probably drop out somewhere en route for a late dinner.

"Right on, guys!" one of their students seconded—and then added, with a knowing wink, Timothy Leary's popular mantra: "*Turn on, tune in, drop out!*"

An hour later, over Maryland crabcakes and chardonnay at a waterfront restaurant just off the Eastern Shore side of the Bay Bridge, "Just what was *that* supposed to mean?" young Mandy pretended to wonder. "What do they think you and I are up to?"

"Making love, not war?" G. suggested or proposed, and raised his glass to hers.

Clink. "I'm ready," M. confessed. "*Been* ready this whole semester, wondering when you'd get around to propositioning me. Your place or mine, Boss?"

Replied George Irving Newett, "Why wait that long? There's a motel right across the highway: I say let's go for it, soon's we're done here."

"And *I* say sooner," countered Amanda Todd, and signaled their server to bring the check, but at G.'s urging agreed to finish their meal and enjoy a celebratory glass of champagne before moving to the Next Stage of their connection. She insisted, moreover, that they either split the cost both of their dinner and of the motel, or else one of them cover the first and the other the other, and that that be their way thenceforward with all shared-experience expenses. "Agreed?"

Agreed. And mildly awkward as it was, after finishing their wine, to check into a motel with no other luggage than Mandy's purse and George's briefcase—no nightclothes, toiletries, or even fresh underwear after their tiring day's march—they eagerly peeled out of their clothing, turned back the bedcovers, and went at it before even washing; again after a joint post-coital shower; and yet a third time in the course of that night, pausing only and briefly before the first of those penile intromissions to address the circumstance of their having brought with them neither male nor female contraceptive devices.

"Withdrawal before ejaculation," had proposed Assistant Professor Todd by nightstand light, opening her lovely smooth thighs to him in the Missionary Position. "Okay?"

"Okay," agreed Full Professor Newett—and so did, not long after. But when they then showered together, returned to bed, re-embraced, and soon found themselves re-aroused, "You might as well know," he informed her, "that with your new playmate, neither withdrawal nor contraceptives are necessary."

"Because you want to knock me up in a hurry?" his bed-partner wondered. "That's a career move we need to discuss first, don't you think?"

"I wish. . . . But the truth is—"

"Let me guess: Is it that you and your late pal Ned," of whom he'd already spoken in numerous of their conversations, "had bilateral vasectomies in your freshman year at Stratford High, to keep from impregnating every coed in class? Or maybe just *you* did, just last week, to keep Shotgun Marriage out of our playbook? How thoughtful of you!" To her new lover's considerable surprise then, *his* new lover bent over him, cupped his scrotum, kissed his already re-tumescing ejaculator (both organs shrouded by her nut-brown hair, worn longer back then than in later years), and crooned, "Poor little spermies, nipped in the bud . . . " To him then, "So: All the way this time, shall we? Fill 'er up?"

"Mandy . . . " Taking her head between his hands as she straddled him: "I never had a vasectomy. Didn't *need* one, it seems. Sorry about that." He lifted her chin; saw her eyes moisten; began to wonder what he was getting himself into, so to speak. "My scribblings are the only offspring I'll ever sire. If you want kids, you'll have to find yourself another stud."

She brushed back her hair. Looked him in the eye. Compressed her lips. Then nodded, wiped her tears on the sheet-edge, and smiled—all this by the afore-noted night-stand illumination, accompanied now by caresses and re-embracement. "Advice perpended, Gee," she said softly. "Meanwhile, if your precious pen is your other penis [G. had showed her the prized black-and-gold Montblanc with which for years he'd first-drafted all his manuscripts], at least they're both *Meisterstücken*. So: Dip your pen in my well, and what we make together is up to our separate muses. Fill 'er up good now, okay?"

Done. And what they then for the first time together made (happily coincident with her first use of his new nickname) was not merely "love" as opposed to "war," but Capital-L Love as distinct from mere though delicious sexual connection: an uppercase blessing that was to be theirs—ever deeper and more richly seasoned, if not necessarily so frequent and athletic—through the forty years from that autumn to the one approaching as G. pens this paragraph. So what if some literal seasons are out of synch with some figurative, and some third-person pronouns fused with first-? What followed that October "springtime" of His/Her/Our conjunction was the prolonged Summer of Our Love—after a tempestuous academic year marked by town/gown confrontations between, on the one hand, the Stratford mayor's office and police department, and on the other a group of student anti-war protestors headquartered in the Shakespeare House for angry demonstrations in town as well as on campus, defused with difficulty by StratColl faculty and administrators (the local National Guard armory being just down the road, fed-up townsfolk agitated in vain for the sort of armed suppression of those rowdy hippies that would lead in 1970 to the Kent State and Jackson State killings). When to all hands' relief Commencement Day finally cleared the campus, the couple were wed in a modest civil ceremony over in Mandy's western-Maryland hometown, attended by their parents and a half-dozen colleagues/friends. They treated themselves to a brief but luxurious-by-their-standards honeymoon tour of Joyce's "Trieste/Zurich/Paris," capped off by a return visit to the same Route 50 motel where they'd first fucked, then set up housekeeping in a newly-rented old clapboard bungalow just off-campus and commenced their married life.

1968: For them it lasted at least until 1975, after Richard Nixon's Watergate-scandaled resignation from the presidency, South Vietnam's surrender to North, and the withdrawal of U.S. troops from that beleaguered country. By then the Woodstock Festival had emblemized another sort of love-summer; American astronauts had landed on the moon, and a not-yet disgraced President Nixon had made landmark diplomatic visits to both Beijing and Moscow. The Senate approved an Equal Rights Amendment banning gender-based pay discrimination*, and the Supreme Court ruled in *Roe v. Wade* against banning abortions in the first two trimesters of pregnancy. For the first time in its history, the Dow-Jones Industrial Average closed above 1000; the military draft ended, and Congress passed (over Nixon's veto) a War Powers bill that curbed the president's authority to initiate overseas military action without its approval. The nation, along with its college and university campuses, largely quieted down; Elvis Presley died, but the Newett/Todds' long Summer summered on. They learned to keep house together; adjusted to each other's ways

---

* Unfortunately defeated in 1982 (Editor Todd reminds Narrator Newett) after a ten-year state-by-state hassle for its ratification.

and routines, their likes, dislikes, and separate histories, sexual and other. With two not-bad academic salaries and no children (more yet to come on that), they were able to buy and renovate the house they'd been renting and turn its spare bedrooms into separate home offices. G. added vegetable-gardening to His several pastimes, and A. flower-gardening to Hers. For three seasons each year they taught their literature classes and writing workshops and served on sundry academic committees; in the long literal summertimes they vacation-traveled in the U.S. and abroad. And for a few hours daily amid all the above, George Irving Newett Montblanc'd his first-draft fictions before editing and transcribing them on his big gray Royal manual typewriter, while Amanda Todd, half a generation ahead of him technologically, composed her verses directly on her handsome IBM Selectric until the advent of desktop computers and word processors. Then, like Eve before Adam, she bit the Apple before her mate, and by the mid-1980s had equipped their home offices with state-of-the-art Macintoshes (although G. preferred still to pen his first drafts).

In the dozenth year of their union—1980, to be precise, by when she'd attained what had been her bridegroom's age at their wedding—she published *her* first-and-thus-far-only book: a small volume of poems from the Johns Hopkins University Press that earned her promotion from the rank of Associate Professor, which she'd held by then for some half-dozen years, to Full. Her husband's long-since-completed second novel, having made its futile rounds of the New York trade houses with some mildly complimentary responses but no takers, was being nudged to no better avail through an ever-diminishing list of smaller, "independent" presses by its author's ever-less-interested agent's ever-changing young assistants. But he still published the occasional short story in this or that quarterly, and was reluctantly adjusting to composition for its own sake and a readership essentially of two. As he had foretold or forewarned, the couple's scribblings were their only offspring. That the "parents" would be those scribblings' all-but-only readers had *not* been by him foreseen: a state of affairs less easily accommodated by a would-be novelist, perhaps, than by a late-twentieth-century poet.

"Trust me," his wife assured him: "You'll get used to it." For it was her conviction, which G. found inarguable, that in the age of video and the Internet, the audience for Literature had grown vanishingly small. "Which doesn't mean . . . " she liked to add, leaving the sentence suspended. And—not blind to the fact that among their contemporaries there were still a few who not only won major literary prizes but even managed on rare occasions to climb briefly onto the best-seller lists—they would shrug and click their wineglasses, or whatever.

Plus, they agreed, although childless they had another category of offspring: their young Shakespeare House workshoppers, who, if not quite disciples (who wanted *disciples*?), were the warmly appreciative mentees of their department's two perhaps-most-popular mentors. "'Twill suffice," Mandy would assure her mate as they cleaned up after one of their end-of-semester parties for those protégés.

Perhaps so. But at times, anyhow, George Irving Newett nevertheless still felt himself to be (and we re-quote him with his permission) "a fucking failure" with both Muse and Mrs.: by no means *impotent* on either front, but infertile, his penned scribblings and penile dribblings equally Dead On Arrival at their respective destinations. Adoption? They briefly pondered it early on, and agreed that like book-reviewing, for example, it was an altogether commendable enterprise—but not for them.

"So what about artificial insemination or in vitro fertilization?" G. half-heartedly suggested in the front end of the 1980s, when "test-tube babies" began making headlines. "All those healthy eggs of yours going down the toilet . . . " To which his wife replied *A,* that for all the two of them knew, her monthly ovulations were no more viable than his twice-or-thrice-weekly ejaculations, and *B,* that even if they were, she wanted nobody's stuff in her private test tube or personal petri dish except her spouse's, thanks. "What the fuck, Gee: We don't even like house pets!"

True. And so it came to pass that by Mandy's menopause in the late 1980s, the subject of Todd/Newett offspring was as comfortably behind them as was any serious hope or expectation of their hitting it big in the poetry-and-fiction way. In the decade to follow (the "Autumn" of their lives and of its present chronicling), when numerous of their Stratford colleagues and neighbors had adult children and young grandchildren to visit or be visited by, the couple will sometimes wistfully pretend the same and speak of "our daughter in Dallas" or "our son in St.

Louis"—even of Amanda's "brother in Buffalo," George's "sister in Seattle," and the similarly alliterative offspring of those nonexistent siblings, the "nephew in New York" and "niece in Naples." But the practice of their deeply-felt shared vocation—more than a hobby, if less than a markedly successful profession—continued, like their sexual connection, to give them much mutual pleasure in and of itself through their lifetime's Summer and beyond.

A season whose end, both literal and figurative, now approaches. The calendric September of its inscribing kicked off with Hurricane Gustav's re-pounding of New Orleans, still struggling to recover from Katrina's devastation three years previously. Having been much criticized for their inattention to that earlier tempest, President Bush and Vice President Cheney canceled their scheduled appearance that day at the Republican National Convention in Minneapolis/St. Paul, where in any case their nationwide unpopularity would have been no asset to the party's about-to-be-nominated candidate, Senator John McCain. Five days later, Tropical Storm Hannah only minimally damaged us East Coasters, but its mid-month Gulf Coast successor, Hurricane Ike, wrecked Galveston, flooded Houston, and left millions powerless along its path to the Great Lakes. . . .

And here we are—*were*, rather, on 9/14/2008: the eve of that year's Harvest Moon, with G.I.N.'s "memoir" of Ned Prosper not much farther along than when he resolved a full season past to write it, and his so-called *Vision #3: 1968* not really a bona fide Vision like its two forerunners, but a mere mini-narrative of his and Mandy's marital "Summer." Which, what the hell, he might as well wrap up: By May 1988, their twentieth wedding anniversary, this childless and siblingless couple were all but parentless as well, having seen both of G.'s through their ripe old age, separate deaths, and interment in the Avon County Cemetery, Amanda's heart-attacked dad through his western Maryland cremation, and her ailing mom into a Stratford assisted-living facility, where her daughter could less inconveniently manage her finances and keep general tabs on her through the brief remainder of her life. Two years later, at the close of academic year 1989/90, the male of this couple accepted with mixed feelings the directorship of StratColl's Shakespeare House Creative Writing Program, in which he had taught by then for nearly three decades: feelings mixed because while he welcomed but didn't really *need* the small salary-increase, he regretted any additional impingement on his writing-time and had long since made clear to his colleagues that he had no particular relish for administrative responsibilities—which however he felt (correctly, it would turn out) he could manage rather better than the program's unimpressive retiring director had done. Appointment effective as of the approaching fall semester, when too the appointee would reach age sixty. Which was and is to say . . .

"The happy ending of our life's long Summer?" Mandy offered eighteen years later, "and its modulation to mellow Autumn? Here's to it."

Yet another clink of what Reader might fairly mistake to be our ever-present wineglasses, although in fact we typically have only one glass at afternoon's end (or, on hot days, gin and tonic on the rocks), perhaps a second (wine only) while preparing dinner together, and a third while eating it: jug wines, mostly, except on such special occasions as toasting the rise of a full Harvest Moon over the Matahannock on a warm mid-September night in the blessedly final year of a ruinous presidential administration, which call for champagne.

"To the year's autumn and ours," her mate seconded—avoiding, as had she, the ominous word *fall*.

"And to your Memoir-Muse?" *his* mate suggested with a smile. "May she wake up already and get with it?"

"Ah, well, Man . . . " G. calls her that sometimes. "I don't know: I think I'm having second thoughts about that whole project. . . . "

And *mirabile dictu*, no sooner did hear himself say *second thoughts* than—transfixed, gazing at the moon with raised champagne-flute in hand—he experienced an unequivocal revelation/sensation, no less strong for its being over in a flash: the for-real

DREAM/VISION/TRANSPORT/WHATEVER #3:
On Second Thought
At first just those words, as if in boldface small capitals and italics, but followed at once by recollection of Ned Prosper's habitually declaring (left thumb up and forefinger extended, as

*mentioned already in Narrator's memoir-notes and -sketches of
his late friend),* "On second *thought . . .* "

   —*"Let's* not *jump off the Matahannock Bridge; let's
go splash Ruthie and her friends instead."*

   —*"Let's* not *add these* Spicy Detective *magazines to the
Boy Scout waste-paper-collection drive; let's squirrel
'em away for later."*

*Et cetera, those Second Thoughts canceling whatever
had preceded them. . . .*

Touching her husband's knee, "You okay?" Mandy wondered.

   G. opened his eyes, realizing only as he did so that he'd
squeezed them shut; exhaled and gave his head a wake-up
shake. "Yeah, yeah. But you know what?"

   "You have my attention."

   "On second thought, to Hell with that memoir project: I'm
a maker-upper, not a tell-aller! Never mind the Story of Ned
Prosper; I'm going to write Ned Prosper's *story*: that novel that
he never got to finish and I never got to read! Autumn, here we
come!"

   As if on cue, at his salute they heard, not summer's "lhude
cuccu," but the season's first flock of migratory Canada geese
honking faintly and then cacophonously downriver: a long V
of them silhouetted against the full moon en route to settling

in nearby creeks and coves. Entranced, the pair watched their passage.

With a sigh, "Autumn, here we *are*," G.'s patient longtime mate then corrected. "Last time I looked I was sixty-five, and a week from now *you'll* turn seventy-eight! Better get on with your Second Thought there, love, and good luck."

second fall?
first fall ii?
this fall?
last . . . ?

Where have all the flowers gone?

I N JUNE OF C.E. 1970, the second year of their marriage, forty-year-old George Irving Newett and his twenty-eight-year-old bride Amanda Todd took out a twenty-year mortgage to buy their first house, the earlier-mentioned white clapboard Stratford bungalow that they'd been renting. To young Mandy especially, the idea that its so-distant pay-out date would ever actually *arrive* was almost amusing: 1990? She nearing fifty, her lively husband sixty, and their life's just-begun Summertime yielding the stage to Fall? Unthinkable! But in a *very* short while, so it seems to them now, that came to pass. Jimmy Carter defeated Gerald Ford, and was himself defeated four years later by Ronald Reagan. The USSR invaded Afghanistan; Mount St. Helens erupted; the space shuttle *Challenger* exploded; President Reagan's reputation, blemished by the Iran-Contra scandal, was re-boosted by four productive summit meetings with Soviet leader Mikhail Gorbachev, presaging an end to the long, apocalypse-threatening Cold War. Et cetera (per *The World Almanac*, which Narrator is obviously consulting)—and in a flash, so it seems in present retrospect, their life's longest season was behind them.

As was this summer of its chronicling, whose wrap-up Harvest Moon coincided with the giant Lehman Brothers Bank filing for bankruptcy, the stock market sinking ever lower, and other signs of a worldwide economic bust ahead. The Newett/Todd "Autumn" that followed—1990–2009—while not *quite* concluded as of G.I.N.'s first-draft penning of it in late November 2008 (*This* Fall? *Second* Fall? *Next* Fall? First Fall II?), has passed even more swiftly, both because its allotted span is a mere nineteen years instead of Summer's twenty-nine ("cold contracts," although '08's autumn thus far has been unseasonably warm) and because time flies faster for us Aging if not-quite-Old-yet Farts. In the *literal* first month after Narrator's equinoctial birthday and first anniversary of his Shakespeare's House head-bang, there was near-panic in world markets as the Dow dropped into the 8000s. Senators Obama and McCain went head-to-head in the presidential campaign

debates; Hurricane Omar, after deflowering the Virgin Islands
with Category 3 winds, fizzled out in the North Atlantic, officially ending the storm season that had jumped its official
starting-gun with Tropical Storm Arthur back in late May.*
And G. I. Newett—remember him?—addressed and daily re-
addressed the unenviable, self-imposed, and admittedly *faute
de mieux* task of dreaming up from virtual scratch the late
Edward "Ned" Prosper's long-lost novel, with little more than
its Shakespearean title to work from: an *in memoriam* instead
of that originally-planned memoir.

Like, uh (he began typing back in early October), maybe
*EVERY THIRD THOUGHT: A Novel by Edward "Ned"
Prosper, by George Irving Newett, by and large?* And for starters, let's see, maybe, "Once upon a time . . . "—or has that
been said somewhere already? But shit: By the October of one's
life as a reader, writer, and professional professor of literature,
what *hasn't* been said already? Tens of thousands of made-up
stories under one's bulging belt, from the earliest oral epics to
last month's "electronic literature" experiments! Enough to set
a chap to musing (on Second Thought, sort of, although without
thinking of it as such) about autumnality in general and in particular one's own, which in G.I.N.'s case Narrator would divide
into two unequal segments: 1) the five too-busy but nonetheless
pleasant years of his Shakespeare Literary House directorship,

---

* Such "seasons" being *merely* official, however, Hurricane Paloma still waits
in the wings to whack Haiti, the Cayman Islands, and Cuba in November, as
Narrator foots this note.

culminating in his 1995 academic retirement, the hand-off of that directorship to popular poet/professor Amanda Todd, and the exchange of their paid-off Stratford digs for a jim-dandy, more easily maintained "coach home" in the Blue Crab Bight subdivision of a new gated community called Heron Bay Estates, a few miles downriver; and 2) the so-far-thirteen years since, leading to Mandy's own approaching retirement at the close of the current academic year* and including, alas, the "pre-fall" to this narrative's First Fall: that infamous late October of 2006, when the Newett/Todds' dear coach home at 1014 Oyster Cove was tornado-trashed by T. S. Giorgio as afore-chronicled, along with most of the rest of Heron Bay Estates. A loss still painful to recollect, and from which, given their age, the couple do not expect ever to *quite* recover, although (thanks largely to House-Manager Mandy) they're managing. . . .

So how's *that* for your big-deal novel's fanfare, *Nedwardio mio*? Okay, okay: We can imagine you, back there in your damned eternal springtime, giving it the finger. But just as the muralist Diego Rivera famously declared, "I paint what I see," so your ex-Muse-Mate—less adventurous than you, but perhaps therefore longer-lived—writes whatever dribbles from his Montblanc, take it or leave it.

Suggested Current Muse-Mate M. on 29 October 2008, the second anniversary of that tornadoing, "I say leave it. This

---

* I.e., June of C.E. 2009. With StratColl's permission, boredom-fearing Professor Todd has scheduled her retirement for age sixty-seven rather than sixty-five.

so-called Second Fall or whatever is more than a third done already, no? Your birthday's a whole month behind us. We've had our first frost; all the leaves are turning, and the U. S. of A. is about to elect its first-ever African-American president, Zeus help him. Seems to me you're overdue for another Capital-V Vision—number four, is it, or have I lost count?"

Number four it would be, if one could have it. Ms. T. hadn't lost count, but her spouse—having lost to the passage of his prime-time season most of his hair and not a little of his libido, general pep, mental acuity, and . . . he forgets what-all else—is clearly also losing his visionality, let's call it. The forehead contusion that occasioned First Fall Vision #1 was long since healed, sans stigmata. Vision #2 had been more or less in synch with the vernal equinox, but #3, such as it was, had arrived a full two months past the summer solstice and (who knew?) might turn out to have been his last.

Almost to his own surprise, *God damn you anyhow, Ned Prosper!* he found himself writing on Wednesday, November 5, the morning after Barack Obama's historic election, which the Todd/Newetts had celebrated with friends at a colleague's large-screen-TV'd house in Stratford's renovated Bridgetown neighborhood. *How is it you never showed and shared your goddamn* Every Third Thought *thing with your oldest/best friend, the way he showed and shared his first novel-in-progress with you, chapter by chapter and draft after draft, and we showed and shared every goddamn other thing, from our naughty fifth-grade "pop-went-the-snaps" poem to each other's adolescent weenies and their post-adolescent adventures? What was so goddamn special about it, to keep it such a goddamn secret? Maybe you realized from Square One that it was a worthless piece of shit, and couldn't admit that your buddy was turning out to be the writer you thought* you'd *be? Or hey: Maybe your big-deal magnum opus didn't actually exist at all! Better yet, on Second goddamn Thought, maybe this is it, right? The Great American Novel, beginning with the immortal invocation/execration "God damn you anyhow, Ned Prosper," lost asshole buddy that George Irving Newett loved almost to the point of bifuckingsexuality! There, he's goddamn said it—or rather,* you've *said it, in this goddamn* Third Thought *thingamafuckingjig that, what the hell, on* Third Thought *might as well kick off with* PRE-AMBLE: CLEARING GEORGE I. NEWETT'S NARRATIVE THROAT *and carry right on to this goddamn "sentence" in goddamn "progress." . . . Why'd you up and die on me, old buddy, and who gives a shit half a century later except, well, obviously, still-desperately-scribbling G. I. Newett, and Mandy'll understand, I hope, bless her: She's what one has instead of kids and grandkids and fame and fortune—well, never mind goddamn fortune, but an undestroyed house anyhow and youthful summertime or at least mid-autumn vigor instead of late-November almost-winterhood, but what the fuck, we Todd/Newett//Newett/Todds have each other plus our separate-and-together scribblings and a (rented) roof over our gray- or scarce-haired heads, the pair of us still "perpendicular and taking nourishment," thank you very goddamn much,*

Zeus-or-whomever, plus writing—who knows, maybe even finishing!—Ned Goddamn Prosper's goddamn Every Third Thought: A Novel in Five Seasons, and there you goddamn have it: THE (by-George) END!

And there *he* (by-George) had it, G. realized/hoped/wished/ decided and declared, first to himself and then—over lunch-time pepperoni-mushroom pizza at Bozzelli's between Mandy-classes—to his mate:

DREAM/VISION/TRANSPORT/WHATEVER #4:
The Great American Goddamn Novel?

Sprinkling extra oregano and hot pepper on her half as she frowned at his page-and-a-half printout, "Nope," his soulmate finally replied, and bit into her first slice.

"Whatcha mean, *nope?* Those pages all but *exploded* out of my pen this morning! I never felt such a *release!*"

"Not even that time in Cancún when we both got dynamite diarrhea? Seriously, Gee: I can see how it must be a Grade-A release—*discharge*, whatever—to put that Third-Thought-Seasons crap behind you—"

"Could you maybe change the terminology?" But he understood at once that, as usual, she was right.

"Sorry there: to *get it off your chest*, okay? But a Vision it isn't. So okay: You've cleared the decks; you've dumped your excess baggage . . . "

"Wiped my butt? Flushed my toilet?"

"*Cleaned your slate*, hon; *settled your accounts.* Thing to do now is refill your pen and turn your page. . . . " With her pizza-free left hand, she flipped the printout facedown on the not-all-that-clean Formica tabletop, displaying its virgin white backside, excuse G.'s imagery. "Take a deep breath. Exhale. Have yourself a *ree*-lax and, Muse willing, not just another hallucination, but a bona fide *inspiration* that'll kick off George Irving Newett's long-awaited *Meisterstück*: the culmination of his career! Sorry to be so stern, love. What're you staring at?"

He was, in fact, while perpending her indeed-stern counsel, focusing on his pages' bare white . . . *verso*, shall we say: not so virginal after all, he pointed out now to On-Target-As-Usual Mandy, but besmirched or anyhow marked with spots of tomato sauce from their booth's previous occupants. A metaphor, maybe, for even the most original and innovative writer's situation? What bard's slate is ever completely clean?

"A poem-worthy point," his wife happily granted, giving him a thumbs-up with her pie-free hand while nudging his leg under-table with her shoe-tip, as was her wont when her husband scored a conversational point. "I'll see what I can do with it back in the shop. And *you'll* see whether you can turn this slop"—by which she appeared to mean, as she handed it back to him, not the pizza-stained *verso*, but the "goddamn"-rich *recto* of his morning's work—"into G. I. Newett's latest." It reminded her, she added as the couple stepped out of the pizzeria, pulling up their coat-collars against a chilly northwest wind, of

Ezra Pound's take-off from Anonymous's "*Sumer is icumen in, / Lhude sing cuccu.*" Did G. remember it?

Winter is icumen in, / Lhude sing Goddamm . . .

"*Raineth drop and staineth slop,*" as Narrator recalled, indicating with a shrug and sigh his blemished script: "*And how the wind doth ramm! Sing: Goddamm!* Pound spells it with two *m*'s and no *n*, as I recollect; I'll do likewise in revision."

Parting at their side-by-side parked cars (Her Honda Civic, His Toyota Corolla, both vehicles in their second olympiad) to go their separate ways—she to the Shakespeare House office that had once been His, he to run a few errands before his cold-weather-afternoon workout in the college gym—they gave their closed right fists a comradely *dap*, Obama-style. Then, "Never mind *re*vision," advised Amanda: "It's time to *en*vision. Take that goddamn *goddamm* and run with it."

Yeah, right. Well. Maybe?

We'll just see.

epi-season post-amble:
"LAST THINGS"

AHEM?
   Okay.

21 December 2008: In Stratford/Bridgetown, autumn's end and winter's beginning. Likewise in the troubled global economy, in George Irving Newett's much-morphed opus-in-"progress," and in its perpetrator's expectable life span. On campus and around the old town and surrounding countryside, all the brilliant maple, birch, and other deciduous leaves have long since fallen except for a few tenacious oak-leaf hangers-on: the sort that, clinging fast right through till spring, reminded old Robert Frost (so Mandy reports) of blown-out-sail shreds on a storm-tossed ship limping into harbor. "He knew there was a Robert Frost poem in that image," she remembers his saying on a visit to her undergrad college shortly before his death, "but he never figured out what it was." Severe winter storms there've been in fact, from Seattle all the way to Frost's New England,

though only a few flurries here in Avon County—where those same Never-Say-Die (or Maybe-We're-Dead?) "survivors" on their gaunt bare boughs put Narrator in mind of the few not-yet-discarded leaves of *Every Third Thought*: the title originally of his lost friend's lost novel, then of G.'s attempted but soon-abandoned memoir of its author, next ("on Second Thought") of his likewise abortive effort somehow to reimagine and recreate that novel itself, and finally—surely *finally*, on Third Thought!—of . . . what? Some *Meisterstück* of his own? A perhaps valedictory but nonetheless fresh, original, inspired, and lively new work by Aged-but-Still-Vigorous Fictionist G. I. Newett? Or merely the remains of a feeble attempt at some such last hurrah?

Re-declares its would-be author, We'll just see.

In the calendar's ten remaining days, the sinking DJIA will waver from just above to just below 8K. Multitudes of workers will lose their jobs in the worst recession since G.I.N.'s childhood, threatening—in his Second Childhood?—to become Great Depression II. The "Big Three" U.S. automakers will plead for a thirty-four-billion-dollar bailout from the federal government. Bernard Madoff's monstrous Ponzi scheme will be revealed to have swindled his investor-clients out of half again that amount. Reduced demand will briefly drop the nation's regular-gasoline price from its October high of more than four dollars a gallon to less than two. And Israel, frustrated by Hamas's escalating rocket attacks from Gaza, will counterattack massively with tanks, bombs, and heavy civilian casualties.

Happy New Year!

We Todd/Newetts will duly salute it—not at midnight on the year's last day, we being early-to-bed types, but with a half-glass of Korbel Brut at maybe 10:15 or so—and toast as well G.'s approaching the final metaphoric season of his life, though presumably by no means the final *calendar* season thereof, he being in good general health and (except for ever-more-frequent "senior moments") some way yet from that Second Childhood, just as the solstice-time we tell of was some way yet from the above-raised Year's End toast. It too we greeted, as is our wont, with a bit of bubbly at sundown on Saturday 12/21: the first half of that bottle whose second (like its sippers, not *quite* fizzled out) we plugged and re-refrigerated until December's end. As is also our wont on such reflective occasions, "Lucky us," we agreed, side by side on our rented "family room" couch in our rented lodgings (owners still undecided about selling, they've reported from south Florida, but definitely tending that way despite the real-estate scene's being currently very much a buyer's market, not a seller's), champagne-flutes in one hand and partner's hand in the other: not only still alive and materially comfortable despite our tornado-loss, but looking back on after-all-pretty-damned-fulfilling careers and a fine life together.

"One suspects," commented Mandy, "that your Dear Reader has heard that already. Maybe more than once?"

"So here's to Him/Her, may She/He fare as well! Here's to your perky poetry and my plodding prose: Long may they waver?"

Lucky to see print at all, opines his Ms., in the age of iPods, BlackBerries, and flat-screen/hi-def/digital TVs, "Just as *we're* lucky to have a roof over our heads and your pension and my salary, plus Social Security both literal and figurative."

"Plus Son in St. Louis and Daughter in Detroit," her mate risked teasing, "or is it Denver? Grandkids in Greenwich and Grenada!"

His mate groaned and let go his hand. "Don't start that again, Gee. We agreed to quit that nonsense."

"So we did: sorry sorry sorry, and sorry to have to keep saying sorry!" But what the fuck, Reader: Now that he'd opened that forbidden door and let chill December in, why not up and confess to her and to Dear Whoever-*You*-Are that "Ned Prosper," too—lost asshole Buddy who steered G. I. Newett through boyhood and young manhood like Virgil tour-guiding Dante through the first two precincts of the Hereafter—has likewise been Narrator's invention all along? . . .

"*What?!*"

. . . That of course one had boyhood pals—a series of them through Bridgetown Elementary, Stratford High, and Tidewater State U.—and the usual initiatory "learning experiences" of one's pre-teens, teens, and early twenties; but none so singly, consistently, *singularly* important as was "Ned Prosper" to "G. I. Newett." Would that one *had* had, and had him still!

To his relieved surprise, instead of emptying her drink on his head and dialing 9-1-1, his wife merely rolled her eyes, drew a deep breath, and asked sarcastically, "To *ménage à trois* with you and me, maybe?" But then added, "No thanks, mate—and you've gotta be kidding that he and his *Third Thought* novel and the rest have been fictions all along, like Son in Schenectady and Daughter in Duluth, or I'm *outta* here!"

He re-took her hand. Smiled. Shook his head. "Nah. Sometimes I half wish they *were*, so I could dream up a *Seasons* novel from scratch. Whether Ned's *fiction* was a fiction, we'll never know for sure. But his being fictitious is *my* dumb-assed, impulsive, God-only-knows-why fiction. The guy himself was flesh-and-blood fact."

Shaking her head, "So you say now. But by our new president-elect's Inauguration Day you'll probably be telling me that *you're him*: that you swam ashore down there in Mexico, deserted the Army, took the name George Irving Newett, and lived happily ever after."

"Hey, I *like* that!"

"Sometimes I really wonder about you, Gee. . . . "

Yes, well: me too.

Another deep breath, exhaled. "Love you anyhow, though."

And me too you.

Presently: "So, then: Are *we* fictitious too, like your made-up stories and my made-up poems? Figments of somebody-or-other's half-assed imagination?"

Shrug: Not for us to say. But from *our* point of view, at least, here we effing are, love, with a few chapters, verses, and seasons yet to go, we hope, before things get grim—including what looks to be a long winter ahead for that president-elect. . . .

"So go write yourself another G. I. Newett novel while the iron's still hot," recommended Amanda Todd. "Or at least lukewarm?" Forefinger against temple, then aimed more or less Geeward: "Like, to begin with, did your maybe-make-believe buddy's Last-Things lists include Last Words, and you could take it from there?"

Glasses empty but bottle still half full, we did indeed then go (next morning) to our separate-but-equal workspaces—where Narrator at His, after thanking once again his Muse of Muses, spent some pleasant December hours recalling and reconstructing a number of those Ned Prosper Last-Things Lists, which he now divided, like the seasons of the year or of one's lifetime, into serial categories. There were, to begin with, his Last Things of Youth, of which several have been mentioned already, and which typically had a twinge of sadness but not regret, they marking also one's commencement to some presumably bigger/ better next thing or stage: Last Year or Day of Studenthood at (Wherever)! Last Academic Degree! Last Day as a Virgin! As a Teenager! As a Bachelor or Bachelorette! By comparison, Ned's Last Things of Mature Adulthood, as he experienced or projected them, had been less exclamatory: Last Day in a particular dwelling-place, job, or town, say, before shifting to some new and presumably better Next, like trading in one's dear old car for its jim-dandy replacement. Last Year or Day of being in one's twenties, one's thirties, forties, fifties. . . . And then, if one lived so long, the Last Things of Later Age, with their more autumnal flavor: last fulltime job; last year before retirement; last *day* on job; last regular salary-check before pension. Last new car. Last house before "downsizing" to assisted-living establishment or nursing home, like Mandy's mom with her daughter's help. (*Who'll help* us? G. wonders parenthetically: *Daughter in Dubrovnik? Son in Siam?*) There were, Ned had noted, things understood in prospect as one got older to be Probably Last, such as In-All-Likelihood-Last Visit to some favorite European country or to one's own country's farther reaches like Alaska and Hawaii—as opposed to such First-Visit-Presumed-To-Be-Lasts as, say, Bora Bora, Tasmania, or Antarctica, none of which N. managed in his abbreviated lifetime nor yet G. as of this re-listing, although who knows, he and Mandy might yet. . . . And contrariwise, those many things not suspected at the time to be Last which however turn out to have been: Last Tennis Game or Ski-Run before knee or shoulder injury rules out for keeps those so-enjoyed sports; Last Sex before petering out, so to speak, into incapacity and/or indifference. Last Get-Together with Whomever before His/Her untimely demise. Last "Normal" Day—felt at the time to be merely ordinary, but in retrospect to have been bliss indeed—before routine physical exam reveals inoperable pancreatic cancer. . . .

And Last G.D. List of G.D. Last Things, okay? Because on Third Thought, who gives a flying fuck?

Well: Old Fart Fictionist George Irving Newett, once upon a time, did in fact give or perhaps receive a Flying Fuck, in the W.C. of a then-new triple-tailed four-engined propeller-driven Lockheed Constellation high over Kansas or maybe Nebraska (on his first-and-only book tour, for his first-and-only published novel), to or from or with Never Mind Whom, he being then between marriages, and rather to his own surprise managed pretty well both that F.F. and that not-yet-O.F.F.'s First Novel, by George, all things considered.

But that's another story, declared G.I.N. to his Montblanc Meisterstück on the New Year's morn, understanding that while his every Third Thought henceforth might be the grave, that still left First and Second Thoughts to get stuff done in—or *on*, whatever. Like, what the hell, maybe a novel about *that*? In, let's say, five "seasons"? Having to do with . . .

He'd just see.

"You do that," seconded Amanda Todd (not aloud, lest she interrupt His musings as he has evidently interrupted Hers, but in effect, by opening the door of His study just enough to wiggle her fingers bye-bye, as she does when stepping out of Hers for a bit on whatever Mandy-errands warrant setting aside her versifying) and followed that "Ta-ta" with her "Back-in-a-bit" *mwah*. . . .

after words:
FIVE POSTSCRIPTIVE SCENARIOS

1. Can You Hear Me Now?

Hello?

Having drafted and more or less edited his latest Whatever and, per house custom, passed the ms. to his Ms. for the judicious, sometimes stern but always on-the-mark critical response that she'll get to in her own good time, Author/Narrator G.I.N. is taking a well-earned breather and, he hopes, refreshing his ever more easily exhausted Muse by touching a few of his favorite literary touchstones, as he inclines to do between projects in hope of re-inspiration by reorientation with those longtime navigation-stars. Also by tending to some not-unimportant domestic and home-office chores.

Anybody there?

In the first of these enterprises, Touchstone Retouching, he has, e.g., reskimmed the first-century C.E. *Satyricon*, by mischievous and lively Petronius Arbiter, both to remind himself

of what the randy Romans were up to when not busy conquer-
ing the known world and to re-salute the progenitor (whether
they knew it or not) of all subsequent comic/satiric prose fic-
tors, from Cervantes, Diderot, Sterne, and Swift down (and he
means *down*) to George Irving Newett. In the same spirit he has
unshelved, wistfully hefted, and respectfully *re*shelved without
reopening his much-but-not-recently-thumbed copy of James
Joyce's *Ulysses*, with index-tabs reverently applied back at mid-
century in a junior-year Modern Lit class at Tidewater State U.
indicating each section's correspondence to a book of Homer's
Odyssey. "Telemachus," "Nestor," "Proteus," "Calypso,"
"Lotophagi," and the rest: G.I.N.'s baptism by total immersion
in the High Modernism that his own literary generation would
find to be a hard act to follow. And he has picked up, put down,
re-picked up, and almost despite himself reread one complete
volume of a two-volume *Arabian Nights* (salvaged, like those
other touchstones, from the remains of his&Mandy's library
in their tornado-wrecked Heron Bay Estates home), impressed
this time less by the Special Effects—magic carpets, magic
words, wish-granting genies in washed-up bottles—than by the
descriptive details of bejeweled palace gates, ugly faces, mer-
chandise for sale by wily merchants in the bazaar. In a word,
texture: never Author Newett's strongest suit. Impressed too, as
always, by Scheherazade's skillful nesting of interlinked tales-
within-tales to save her life and rescue the king from his mur-
derous, kingdom-wrecking misogyny—the way G.I.N. nests
parentheses within dashes within serial subordinate clauses as

if to postpone ending the sentence in progress and having to begin another. In S.'s case, *Entertain me or die!* In G.'s case . . .

Don't ask.

Whether all this ritual re-touchment will re-inspire or re-discourage the toucher remains to be seen.

How touching.

As for Enterprise Two, those not-unimportant domestic and home-office chores: Author/Narrator is not a *complete* technological illiterate, but he's a decidedly Senior Citizen who, over the decades between the Great Depression of the 1930s and the current global economic slump (2009 and counting), has graduated from manual to electric typewriters, thence through a series of ever less clunky, ever faster and more sophisticated desktop computers (used in this household only for word-processing, e-mail, a bit of Internet browsing, and simple home-office spreadsheets; never for video games, movie-watching, music-downloading, news-reading, "blogging," and the like). At his age and stage he can be excused, he trusts, for lamenting the need to replace his also-aging, possibly storm-damaged, anyhow now dead "old" Apple iMac (bought a mere nine years ago!) with its new state-of-the-art flat-screen counterpart in the first year of Barack Obama's presidency, when one was lucky to be a pensioned-off academic in a modest but suburban low-rise condominium on Maryland's Eastern Shore instead of a laid-off thirty-something trying to meet mortgage- and kids' tuition-payments. He and Mandy have done their bite-the-bullet bit for the economy, he reckons, by replacing not only his "old" computer but his "old" cell phone as well (popped off his belt-clip, evidently, while he and Ms. Missus—currently at work in her minimal home office across the hallway from his—were bicycling a few weeks ago in nearby Stratford and the adjacent Matahannock riverside park). One hopefully supposes that even a Fart too Old for iPods, MP3s, BlackBerries, Palm Pilots (and whatever high-tech gadgets will have already replaced those by when anybody reads this list) will eventually get the hang of these two new purchases, as he quite got the hang, if by no means mastered the full capabilities, of their predecessors. For the present, however, he's overwhelmed by all their bells and whistles: so *many* applications, each with its array of options and settings! And the two hypergadgets *interlinked* (or at least interlinkable, he gathers, according to their respective User's Manuals), as their predecessors were not. Why would one's computer desire intercourse with one's mobile phone, and vice versa? Ah: because the latter isn't just a telephone these days, like its lost predecessor and Mandy's fortunately-still-with-us "old" one, but also a camera (as is the computer too, Zeus help us, he now discovers!), a text-messager, and half a dozen—maybe a dozen and a half—other things as well, whose "files" his computer may want or need to "access" and conversely (or *perversely*), if he ever learns how to apply those applications.

Get him outta here!

No, don't bother: At age all-but-fourscore, he'll *be* outta here soon enough. Meanwhile, with an ever-shifting mix of dismissive annoyance, curiosity, exasperation, fascination, and frustration, in the morning hours officially reserved for muse- and home-office deskwork he has found himself tinkering with these intricate new toys. And it's in the course of his fiddling-with/exploring/trying-out/fucking-up their miscegenative interconnections—Googling the time-differential, e.g., between Maryland and Morocco* while still linked to the cell phone via some wireless technology that he hasn't read up on yet in the manuals—that he first hears her voice:

Hello.

A woman's voice, neither old nor young by the sound of it: a serious but pleasant, mature female voice from somewhere in the space between computer (on hutch desktop along one wall of home-office/study, the area G. calls "Production") and cell phone (temporarily on "Business" work-table on opposite wall, along with cordless phone, desk calendar, file drawer, and the like): i.e., in the "Creation" workspace where he longhands the first drafts of his O.F. Fictions and where—but *from* where? Digital weather-alert radio? Electric pencil sharpener?—he hears that voice again, this time interrogatively:

Anybody there?

"Sometimes I wonder that myself," he admits to himself or whomever. Could it be Mandy, maybe, calling his new cell phone from hers, or from the cordless on her desk? Not likely she'd do that before he's finished with its set-up and ready for a test call.

---

* The Todd/Newetts' thus-far-only venture into Islam, of which his recent revisit to Scheherazade's *Nights* has pungently reminded him: a memorable summer visit to Tangier back in the 1980s.

Anyhow, she's busy with her Muse just now, he assumes, as her husband would rather be with his than futzing around like this. But now that he's into it, he's more or less hooked.

Can you hear me now?

The classic cell-phoner's question—and that really *does* sound like Amanda's voice, sort of, but as if she's mimicking some outsourced tech-support service person in Mumbai, or speaking in italics.

"Well," he says aloud this time—and mighty odd it feels, as if speaking aloud to himself—"I hear *somebody*. The question is who—or *whom*, I guess—and from where? Can *you* hear *me*?"

No reply, so he supposes not—and screw this: He'll go take a piss, replenish his coffee, and update Mandy on his non-progress with their new gadgets. But having bladder-voided, flushed, rezipped, and washed hands for the second or third time since daybreak (a bi-hourly rite among enlarged-prostate-near-octogenarians, its last step given particular attention in the current swine-flu scare), he finds to his mild surprise his wife's study unoccupied: door open instead of ajar, desk lamp off, and computer dark, as they would not normally be if she were, e.g., merely visiting their other bathroom. Nor does he find her in the kitchen when he refills his thermal mug and turns the auto-drip percolator off for the day.

"Mandy?"

Probably putting some paid bill in the mail. Or maybe—it being a sunnybright and breezeless tidewater morning, mild for mid-March—even musing with her notebook out on the condo's riverfront pier, as she sometimes enjoys doing. Come (belatedly) to think of it, didn't she finger-wave him a See You Later not long since? En route back from the kitchen, he detours to their living room's river-facing windows: no sign of her down there. So okay, she's somewhere between—in conversation, maybe, with a neighbor also posting mail at the building's communal mail-drop, or scanning the community notice-board beside it. No problem, for pity's sake, and he knows she wishes he didn't fret so whenever he briefly loses track of her (not that he frets *much*, but still . . .), just as *he* wishes she'd let him know when she's stepping outside for a bit or otherwise getting temporarily out of touch, the way he routinely keeps *her* posted on *his* movements even at the risk of interrupting her musings. Okay, so this time she did that, if he remembers correctly— but how often, shopping together in supermarket or department store, he'll turn from whatever wares he's been regarding and find her vanished, whom he'd thought close by! Then the systematic look down each aisle and section, from Produce to Dairy, Men's Wear to Jewelry, until he locates her—sometimes *not* locating her until the second check, she perhaps happening to round one end of an aisle as he rounds its other, or he perhaps not spotting her behind some other shoppers. "Why does it *bother* you so?" she'll ask: "If we happen to get separated, just wait for me at the check out." He *is* a bit obsessive about it, he'll acknowledge, to the point even of bad dreams on that theme: losing her not in the Stratford Safeway or Walgreens, but in the swarming Tangier *souk*, say, where an otherwise appealing little beggar-waif whose guide-services we'd politely declined had trailed after us calling *"Dur-r-ty Chews! Dur-r-ty Chews!"*—as if all guideless non-Muslim tourists were *ipso facto* Jewish and *ipso facto* et cetera. But it was in Tangier also—the city that inspired Rimsky-Korsakov's *Scheherazade* suite and Matisse's odalisque paintings—that G. I. Newett had felt closest to his favorite storyteller, especially at evening prayer-call time, when the muezzins summoned the faithful with amplified chants from the lighted minarets of mosques near the Newett/Todds' hotel.

"You didn't *used* to get so worked up about it," his mate will scold when he finally finds her, or reports yet another such alarming dream. So clearly now can he hear her saying that, half amused and half chiding, it's as if that computer/cell phone/ whatever has spoken again.

"That's because I didn't used to be an Old Fart," he'll acknowledge, granting readily that the source of this prevailingly mild Separation Anxiety is no doubt his ever-growing awareness of the actuarial clock: that their so-blessed life together is mostly behind them, and that any year now, any semester (their academic-reflexive calendar measure), any *day*, really . . .

Mandy?

Is it *his* voice speaking that dear name as if in italics, or the cell phone/computer's, or no literally audible voice at all, but the italicized next line of some new Newett-work in uncertain progress that goes on to say *Pretend you just want to tell her to come listen to this weirdo Genie-thing in your study—which in fact you do want her to—and go check every room in the place again, plus walk-in closets, balcony, outside corridor, stairwell to the ground floor, garage, parking lot—the works. Then when you find her coming back from putting out the garbage or whatever, you'll feel enormously relieved and pathologically stupid.*

Not a bad idea. And if I don't?

Don't find her, you mean, or don't go looking, but for a change assume the best and likeliest scenario rather than the worst/unlikeliest, and just sit there and type out more G. I. Newett-sentences, maybe in a less paranoid, self-titillative vein?

"Genie-thing," he sees he's written (not on that still-unfamiliar new word-processor, but with his faithful old fountain pen, a comfort to return to). Along with the djinns/jinnis/genies of the *Nights*, the word conjures his beloved's long-since-discarded middle name. *Amanda Jean Todd*, her parents dubbed her, and although by the time G. met her she had long since dropped the "Jean" (on the grounds that double first names like "Barbara Ann," "Susie Mae," and "Amanda Jean" sounded redneck to her), he sometimes teases her with it still: "My wonder-working Jeannie," he'd call her in their relationship's early years, when her mere touch sometimes gave him an erection; or, stroking her pubes, "My Genie with the light brown hair." Or—when he had introduced her to the *Nights*, with their varying transliterations of the Arabic word for those plot-escalating spirits—"Me G.I.N.; you Jinni: *Open Sesame*, sez me, and your devoted Ifrit will gladly enter."

Stuff like that. Those were the days—not that these latter ones aren't sweet, rich, precious. *Desperately* precious—there's the rub, for the actuarial reasons aforementioned—and damn it to hell, why doesn't he cap his fucking pen, stop imagining or pretending that he's hearing voices, stop scaring himself shitless that his Without-Whom-Nothing mightn't be where she normally is at this weekday hour or that it's Bad News if she happens not to be, and *just go have a look* instead of imagining that he's done that already, in vain?

"Hey, Mandy? Come listen to this. *Mandy?*"

Did you speak that aloud, or just write it?

2. Are You There?

Well of *course* she's not in her study/workroom composing Mandy-verses, paying bills, making service-people appointments, and/or arranging the next Todd/Newett vacation trip (to Alaska, he believes it's to be, next August): When G. exits his to get a swig from his personal spring-water bottle in the fridge, he notices that hers—a different brand, for ID purposes, although they usually refill each a few times from a gallon jug on the countertop before discarding—isn't there. Gone also is their grocery-and-errand list from under its magnet on the fridge door and, when he now checks, the blue plastic ice-packs from the freezer door shelf and the small portable cooler from the laundry room that they always take to the supermarket. So okay: That means that her car will be gone too, from its numbered space behind the condo, because—of course!—she had business on campus, including (as he now more or less remembers) lunch with the guy who succeeded her as Director of Stratford College's Shakespeare House upon her retirement. How could he have forgotten? It's probably even noted on his desk calendar, and she didn't interrupt him to remind him because she assumed he was communing with the Muse of O.F. Fiction, not futzing with computer/cell-phone interlinkages, and she decided to pick up a few items at the market while she was in town: a chore that her mate much enjoys sharing with her except for those occasional Where-did-she-go? moments aforementioned. So relax! Not to worry! Write a sentence!

Or push a few buttons. . . .

Are you there?

I'm here, Genie-lady. Where're you? And *who*?

I'm here, as you can hear.

Here where?

Wherever here is. *As to* who, *well* . . . *Who's anybody? Who's "who"? Who's You?*

G. I. Newett, as if you didn't know it: Look him up in the Who's Who of Postmortem Fiction.

Postmortem? . . .

All that Death-of-the-Novel crap, you know? Very big in late-twentieth-century English departments. 'Twas *born* a-dying, I've heard tell, like Yours Truly and the rest of us; been dying vigorously ever since, and can be expected to go on dying for a lively while yet. Over?

But you just said that it's not over.

You know what I mean: Your turn now.

To die? Not my métier, *friend: As you may have read, we genie-types can sometimes be tricked back into our bottles, but we're afflicted with immortality.*

"Afflicted," you say? Is it maybe contagious, then? Sexually transmissible?

Listen to you!

I'm listening to *you,* Dreamy Jeannie.

Your beloved bed- and life-mate of forty years steps out of the house for a couple of hours, and you flirt with your fucking office equipment!

Provocative modifier noted. As some other oldie once said about his latter years, "Sex goes. Memory goes. But the memory of sex never goes."

Spare us the details.

"Us" meaning, presumably, G. I. Newett's uncorked jinni/djinn/genie and his Patient Reader, should any such exist. To spare herself the details, perhaps, Ms. Jeannie-Voice goes on to remind him that increasingly of late, when his mate is out of the house or even just unexpectedly out of sight, G. I. Newett inclines to more or less alarming What Ifs. What if she's taken a tumble down the condo stairs (less likely at her age than at his), or had an out-of-nowhere ruptured aneurysm? What if she and her pesto-green Honda Civic are carjacked in the Safeway parking lot (such things can happen, even in low-crime Stratford/Bridgetown), or rammed by an errant driver, or squashed by a falling tree such as they sometimes see along Avon County's rural roads?

Come off it: More likely she's hooking up with some StratColleague because your paranoia's been driving her bananas—or your recent inclination to conjure up sexy genies.

Sexy, are you?

Forget about it.

He does, for the present anyhow, and scribbles instead his resolve, when Mandy attends the two-day Eastern Shore Writers Association Conference—scheduled for this weekend, is it? down at Marshyhope State U.?—to abstain from such grim and admittedly far-out (but not *unimaginable*, Q.E.D.) worry-wart worries. They are, he acknowledges, inspired not by love alone, but also by self-concern: his practical as well as emotional dependence upon his mate in so many life-departments, from loving companionship and moral/ethical compass-correction to menu-planning, bill-paying, copyediting, laundry—the works. He does his share, he hopes: managing as best he can their uncomplicated finances and home-office accounting; vacuuming the floors before she does all the rest of the weekly cleaning; handling a few guy-type things like car tire-pressure and fluid-level checks and simple household repair-and-maintenance chores; serving as her *sous-chef* in the kitchen—but although neither of them can imagine life without the other, he believes (despite her ardent, exclamatory denials!) that in the dreadful event, she would somehow cope better than he. At their age, needless to say, they've seen friends and colleagues aplenty widowed or widowered—some

by fluke accidents like those afore-imagined, others by merci-
fully brief or painfully extended illness, and at least one by her
spouse's alcoholic suicide. Remarkably, to us Newett/Todds,
the survivors seem in the main to carry on, thanks no doubt to
networks of supportive friends and family-members. Although a
few succumb to chronic depression, most of their acquaintance,
aided by their grown children, stoically exchange their houses
for apartments or assisted-living quarters, sometimes in a different part of the country. They attend social-club events, do volun-
teer work, and in a few cases even remarry. Unimaginable!

*Even for a bloke whose line of work is imagining stuff, like
sexy "Jeannie"-voices in his workroom? Conveniently coincident with the non-presence, let's say, of his Without-Whom-
Nothing mate?*

May one inquire just what the fuck you're suggesting?

*One may. You having conjured my Mandy-like voice out
of these office-gadget interlinkages into your quote "Creation
Space" unquote, I'm suggesting that you now take advantage
of Ms. M.'s presumably temporary absence to conjure into
your Business Space my also-temporary but (literally) fabulous
physical presence: naked as a jaybird, slim and frisky as your
mate was back when the pair of you first frisked—but with
darker hair, I guess, we Jeannies being of Persian/Arabic ex-
traction—and we'll get down to Business, me straddling your
magically restored youthful virility with my pert young bub-
bies in your face and humping your geriatric brains out. Or in,
rather, until you're ready to fire off not yet another O.F.F., but*

a B.&B.T.D.F.: Brash and Brilliant Tour De Force! When wifey then returns from her in-town and on-campus business (if she ever does, and if that's where she is and what she's up to), you'll surprise her with a very different sort of Capital-P Performance from the ones you've been laying on her lately. Whatcha say, Boss? Come have yourself one last Capital-V Vision!

Well: Since you ask, I say *A,* that I've never understood why we say "naked as a jaybird," when every jay *I've* ever seen has head-to-tail plumage. . . .

Until we're plucked. Shall we get to it?

And *B,* that that's quite enough Old Fart Fantasizing for today. Back into the bottle you go, girl: I'm off to meet Mandy for lunch at Bozzelli's and do our weekly grocery shopping.

Quit fooling yourself.

Quit fooling *your*self, George Irving Newett says or writes, whether to "her" or to himself or to both or neither. *She's out checking the mailbox; back in a minute. She's doing stuff in town; back after lunch. She's prepping her poetry reading for the Shore Writers conference* (which, despite his pride and pleasure in her verse, he has reluctantly decided not to attend, because its venue evokes so many bittersweet memories of his brief first marriage). Or none of the above?

For the first time, he uses his new cell phone to dial hers—and gets her voicemail voice, as reminiscent of "Jeannie's" as was *her* voice of his wife's:

Please leave a message after the tone.

"Mandy? Where *are* you? Sweetheart?"

3. Hello?

"An instrument of Satan," Mark Twain called Samuel F. B. Morse's newly-invented telephone. George Irving Newett inclines to agree, granting however that like other of the Devil's bright ideas—television, the Internet, alcohol, human curiosity and imagination—it has its virtues, to the point of near-indispensability. Himself rather a telephonophobe, more inclined to exchange e-mail messages with friends and colleagues than to dial them up, and appalled by the hosts of cell phone chatterers on the street and in shops, restaurants, and stadiums (not to mention driving vehicles!), he nonetheless grants the superior closeness of phone calls over written messages. *Closerness*, rather, to face-to-face conversation: the audible voice, the spontaneous give and take. He's thankful that videophones never caught on back in the twentieth century, as many believed they would, and he quite understands the popularity of Facebook, YouTube, and suchlike audiovisual intercommunication among twenty-first-century young folk—but not for him, thanks. Like the desktop computer in his study's Production area, the telephone in its Business area and others here and there in the Todd/Newett condominium are instruments of home and home-office business: G.I.N. doesn't turn to them for pleasure.

Not even if Jeannie With the Light Brown Pubic Hair pops out of them to let Pop pop her?

Especially in that unimaginable unlikelihood.

Which however he seems lately to have managed to imagine, in his absent mate's recent absences.

Shame on him for that—but he here reminds all hands that Creative Imaginings are as non-responsible as dreams. It's what one *does* with them that matters.

So let's see what we can do! Come do me, Pops. . . .

He further reminds all hands (himself especially) that his Mandy's "absence" is not indefinite, as to either whereabouts or duration: She's attending ESWAC, the annual Eastern Shore Writers Association Conference, down at Marshyhope State University on the lower Shore, remember? Where more than half a century ago George Irving Newett commenced his academic-pedagogical career as an entry-level Instructor of English Composition.

You wish . . .

What Narrator wishes is that either his wife were back up here with him (as she was supposed to be by now, and no doubt soon will be: weekend traffic delays, most likely; you'd think she'd've called—but he knows she knows he dislikes phone-calls) or he down there with her—preferably the former. Hates eating and sleeping alone; making up their king bed single-handed in the morning; fixing meals and watching TV by himself, here where they do just about everything together except on the toilet and in their workrooms! He *much* wishes now that he'd gone down to Marshyhope with her, but—

But much as you honor your long-ago-failed first matrimonial adventure with Miz Marsha Green, you still find its mise-en-scène *off-putting, blah blah blah. Let's not go there, okay?*

I didn't—and so now I get the bill. But Mandy'll be back anytime now, so forget it. She's just a bit late, is all.

You wish. Meanwhile, I believe you mentioned quote, going down, unquote?

And *you* mentioned "light brown hair." I thought you'd said your hair was dark?

Better check it out, don't you think? Even by your wishful-thinking timetable, we've got awhile to frisk: Come find my G-spot!

Back into the bottle you go, girl: If you'd caught me between matrimonial chapters four decades ago, we would no doubt have checked each other out for sure. But alas, we didn't have cell phones and computers back then to interbreed and interbreed with, and now Yours Truly isn't yours except in bored/restless/fretful/sportive/time-filling/make-pretend conversation, he being a long-happily-and-faithfully-married Oldster who *very* much misses his Missus.

And who ain't seen nothing yet—either of Jeannie in the Light Tan Flesh or of really missing his late Miz Mandy.

"Really" missing? Just what the F-blank-blank-blank is that "really" supposed to mean? And that "late"?

. . .

Well?

. . .

Hello?

. . .

Hey, damn it: I'm talking to you! Hello? *Hello?*

. . .

4. Djinn and Tonic

When one's life-partner of nearly half a century, homeward bound from a minor writers' conference that she self-teasingly labeled Conference of Minor Writers, is suddenly and altogether unexpectedly taken from one—by head-on collision of pesto-green Honda Civic, say, with momentarily out-of-control silver/bronze GMC Sierra 4 × 4 pickup truck whose middle-aged driver suffers cardiac arrest at 55 mph on Avon County Road 444 just outside Stratford town limits and also dies, either in or immediately prior to crash (Who cares which? And how one's late poet/professor/life-partner Amanda [Jean] Todd used to wince at *her* life-partner's inclination to the impersonal pronoun "one"; and how one's heart, soul, and gut now wrench at the memory of her editorial acumen, among a thousand other memories!)—one can be excused (one presumes, but doesn't finally give a shit) for hitting the bottle a bit beyond one's routine, afore-specified three drinks a day (see "Summer," p. 135 *supra*).

Or for indulging even *more* than a bit beyond that customary quota. In deep shock since the so-often-darkly-fantasized-and-feared phone-call (County Sheriff's Office, regretfully reporting EMS transport of accident-victim to Avon Medical Center and confirmation of her death—and how Mandy also winced at her spouse's hyphenated adjectival strings!), G. I. Newett is astonished at his somehow managing to address, through the following season, the all but endless postmortem To Do list—or *would* be, were he capable in his new circumstances of astonishment or any other feeling beyond stunned devastation. There is, e.g., the

—Clerical Stuff, into which the Newett/Todds were initiated by the serial demises of their parents over the decades, Mandy as usual managing most of it. Death certificates to be filled out and multi-copied; notification of medical and life insurers, credit card companies, Social Security Administration and other pension and annuity payers; execution of Last Wills & Testaments, etc. etc. Then the

—Notification of Relatives (in their case, none) and of Friends and Colleagues, who'll no doubt plan a memorial service at Shakespeare House for their much-esteemed colleague that he'll have to steel himself to attend unless he preventively slits his wrists or flings himself off the Matahannock River Bridge on an outgoing tide, as a graduating StratColl senior once unaccountably did and G. I. Newett wishes he could fucking do as well. Plus the

—Funeral Arrangements: As with the clerical shit, he's had some previous experience with the folk at the local "parlor" upon the "passing," as they like to call it in the trade, of those elder Todds and Newetts—Mandy mainly in charge here too, she being the abler hand at more things than not. Casket and headstone selection; funeral service and interment in Avon County Cemetery per deceased's expressed wishes; help with survivor's accommodation to radically altered circumstances, etc. etc. He and Mandy being childless and siblingless non-believers who in recent years have almost never bothered even to visit their progenitors' graves (contenting themselves instead with marking the respective birth- and death-days with commemorative candles lighted on dining room table beside framed photos of the deceased), the Arrangements for his *Sine Qua Non* will come down to little more than

—Disposal of Corpse—via cremation, by their longstanding agreement. "Cremains" to be not ceremonially urned or ritually scattered, as sundry of their bereaved colleagues have done with the leftovers of their Dear Departeds, but dumped by the Parlor People, neither he nor Mandy being sentimental *re* the ashes of a once-so-treasured body. And then . . .

—Disposal of Deceased's Personal Effects. Aiaiai! Oyoyoyoy! With Ma and Pa Newett and Pa and Ma Todd, an affecting (and mighty labor-intensive) chore: taking a few small mementoes for themselves; donating closet- and dresser-drawerfulls of clothing to charity-places; arranging and presiding over estate sale of furniture, housewares, wall art, cars, real estate. But in the case of one's so-much-Better half . . . unthinkable! Empty her clothes closet? Sell or donate the king bed in which for decades they royally disported, and in their later age still long and lovingly embraced at each day's and night's commencement? Her files of finished and unfinished poems, prized lecture-notes, and correspondence with fellow scribblers and former students, together with the dear desk at which she did her muse- and schoolwork? He'd rather dump himself!

Not a bad idea, come (again) to think of it.

Come again? Let's get to it, Gin-boy!

You again. Where were you when I called you, at the end of Scenario Three?

Back in our namesake bottle, I reckon—which one gathers you've reopened for sorrow-drowning purposes. Good mourning, Comrade Newett!

Okay, we get it: G.I.N./Djinn/Gilbey's Dry. Which in fact Yours Truly has re-resorted to lately in this bleakest of his life's seasons. So?

The classic Old Fart Final Solution: OFF yourself with alcohol, meanwhile indulging last-ditch gin-fueled fantasies. . . .

Djinn-fueled? Who do you think you're fueling?

It's whom, as a former English teacher should know, and as his quote/unquote "late" mate would for sure. Whom do you think you're fooling?

With these progressively Worse-to-Worst case Scenarios, do you mean, or with the virtual materialization of presumably nubile, presumably lovely and buck-naked *Arabian-Nights*-like Genie from cell phone/computer coupling? And why do we say "buck naked," when every male Virginia White-Tail *I've* ever seen is as furred from horn to hoof as "jaybirds" are feathered from beak to tail?

And even your bare-naked "Jeannie," as afore-noted, is light-brown-haired where it matters. Come have a look.

. . .

Has she mentioned that her nom de plume—nom de tongue, I guess, since she's a story-teller, not a story-penner—happens to be "Scheherazade," and that all those yarns she spun in the Thousand and One Nights *are just a drop in her narrative bucket? One jigger from the Jinni's bottle? So come jigger me, Boss: Dip your pen in my well, the way King Shahryar used to do every fucking Arabian night! Amuse and re-muse yourself, and I'll turn a Narrative Old Fart into the Still-Potent Pop of Postmortem Prose Fiction!*

To which genre, come to think of it, this Scenario in particular might be said to belong. Or maybe *Premortem* Pre-emission Premonition? Prophylactic Imagining of the Unimaginable?

You wish. You hope. You'd pray, were you the praying sort. No condoms needed with us Jeannies, by the way—and by the way, have you ever heard of Auditory Ejaculation?

Can't say I have. Why do you ask?

Because, being less sozzled than some on Djinn and Tonic, I'm pretty sure I hear someone coming. Better shut down your pornophonic play-toys now, before she catches you in the Acting-Out act. Assalamu alaikum, hasta la vista *dot dot dot?*

. . . !

5. The Book of Fourteen Thousand Six Hundred-Plus Nights

The *likeliest* scenario, of course, is that Amanda [Jean] Todd is asleep beside George Irving Newett on her side of their matrimonial bed, as she's been for all but a few of their union's forty yearsworth of nights. Even Middle-of-the-Night Paranoid Fantasizers like G.I.N.—whether fetched from sleep by his aging bladder or just wakened, more or less, from a particularly vivid series of brief but alarming dreams—would grant as much. Windows, blinds, and curtains closed, their bedroom is entirely dark except for the night-lighted slit from not-quite-closed bathroom door that guides them several times per night to urinary relief, each of them usually sleeping through the other's exits and re-entrances. Unless he switches his bedside light on (which of course he won't), he can't always be sure she's there beside him even if he turns and looks. Which he's not about to do, *A,* because he's not quite *that* paranoid, yet; *B,* because even if she's not there, all it would mean is that she's off a-peeing; and *C,* because he's lying comfortably (except for his own gradually increasing bladder-signals) in his usual position—right-side down on his bed-side, facing away from his beloved—and dreaming up all this Scare-Yourself-Shitless shit.

Reader is here informed that we Todd/Newetts don't flush toilets at night, lest we wake our mate. G. listens for her tell-tale tinkle—which, however, he doesn't inevitably hear, his auditory acuity (too) being Not What It Used To Be. Nor does he hear his partner respiring beside him—always a comfort even when she's lightly snoring, as both occasionally do—or having one of her Chuckle Dreams, which it makes him smile to hear, or one of her Whimper Dreams, which it so hurts his heart to hear that he sometimes has to touch her hip or shoulder to interrupt it, a usually effective tactic. Nor has he for some while now felt any stirrings from her side. . . .

So what? So she's sleeping comfortably but less than deeply: i.e., quietly. All he needs to do, for crying out loud*, is turn over and look or feel—or cry out loud, thereby relieving his nutcase apprehensions at cost of her well-earned rest. (He almost said *peaceful* rest—as in R.I.P.? Caught himself just in time, but finds himself writing it here instead.)

Hell with that: He'll know soon enough, when he hauls out to do his Number Two Number One, whether his bed-partner of some 14,600+ nights is where of course of course of course of *course* she'll be: right there beside him. Or else busy doing what he, not having heard her go before him, will have gotten up to do. Or . . .

Or gone before him, Zeus forefend, as more and more of their coevals' mates have done, and as he well knows (but can't finally imagine, and therefore finds himself almost obsessively trying to) that she or he—may it be *he*, he selfishly but fervently wishes!—must likewise do. Or has already done, as sooner or later he'll have to admit if never accept that she's done already, damn her bless her bring her back or get him out of here!

You could, you know, just turn the fuck over, reach out, and touch, instead of playing these stupid games.

I know. I know.

So do it, and I'm outta here for good.

---

* Another odd locution that, having heard himself think it, Narrator supposes must be euphemistic for "for Christ's sake." He'll Google it in the morning, after breakfast and before getting back to his Old Fart Ficting—always assuming, dot dot dot . . .

It's about time.

What isn't? C'mon, Gee-man: One . . . Two . . . Three? *Or on Second Thought, as your alledgedly late pal would say, how about*

Three *(our little* ménage à trois*)?* . . .

Two *(you Todd/Newett//Newett/Todds)?* . . .

One? *(Reach out and touch, old sport, and our story's done).*

.

Printed in the United States
by Baker & Taylor Publisher Services